Postcards from Patmos

Postcards from Patmos

Visions and Letters of an Exiled Prophet

Osvaldo D. Vena

FOREWORD BY
Charles H. Cosgrove

RESOURCE *Publications* · Eugene, Oregon

POSTCARDS FROM PATMOS
Visions and Letters of an Exiled Prophet

Resource Publications
An Imprint of Wipf and Stock Publishers
199 W. 8th Ave., Suite 3
Eugene, OR 97401

www.wipfandstock.com

PAPERBACK ISBN: 979-8-3852-3093-8
HARDCOVER ISBN: 979-8-3852-3094-5
EBOOK ISBN: 979-8-3852-3095-2

VERSION NUMBER 10/17/24

To Alva Caldwell, friend and colleague

Contents

Foreword

In *Postcards from Patmos*, Dr. Osvaldo Vena completes a trilogy of books in which he adopts the voices of ancient figures of Christianity's earliest days and tells their stories in vivid autobiographical narratives. *Postcards from Egypt*, the first book of this series, imagines that Jesus survived the crucifixion and escaped to Egypt, where he wrote a memoir looking back on his life, commenting, not always approvingly, on the beliefs and practices of those who carried out missions in his name across the Mediterranean world. In a second book, *Postcards from Rome*, Vena speaks as the Apostle Paul during the last phase of his mission, where Paul pens an autobiographical letter in which he shares his experiences, commitments, anxieties, and hopes.

Postcards from Patmos, the third and final book of the series, features John, author of the Book of Revelation. But unlike the other two books in the *Postcards* series, which represent their subjects looking back on their lives from the perspective of old age, John speaks in *Postcards from Patmos* about a singular event, a mystical experience that occurred while he was in exile on the island of Patmos. He received a series of extraordinary visions, which he recorded in the Book of Revelation. Now he rehearses them for a fresh audience—*us*.

In this retelling, John expresses his own feelings about what he saw and heard, and gives explanations of the meanings of the strange scenes he was shown, scenes he figured out only bit by bit as they unfolded. John also suggests parallels between the visions granted to him and the world of the twenty-first century. Parallels, not predictions. It has been common in many Christian circles to assume that Revelation predicts the future "end times" and that the task of the church is to figure out what exactly is predicted and when it is to occur. The temptation has been for each generation of Christians to conclude that they must be living in the end times, whether they lived in the tenth century (when Europeans went almost mad as the first millennium came to a close), the fifteenth (when the Protestant Reformation sparked a great deal of apocalyptic excitement), the nineteenth (when the very elaborate future eschatology of Dispensationalism was born), the twentieth (when supposed End-of-the World dates came and went), or the twenty-first (when many people are still confident that they can finally and accurately decipher the predictions encoded in biblical prophecy). This approach to Revelation is in many ways a very arrogant exercise in fantasy, since it encourages people to think that although every prior generation was *not* the generation about which the Bible speaks in prophecy, they themselves belong to that last generation and that only Christians like themselves are in the know, while everyone else is clueless and deluded.

This approach has also led to many disappointments, generation by generation, since claims made by preachers and popular Christian books that the End is about to take place go unfulfilled. Predicted dates pass; the world goes on. Some of us grew up in a time when Dispensationalist preachers declared, without a hint of uncertainty, that the establishment of the State of Israel in 1948 marked the beginning of the last generation, meaning that the world as we know it would come to a dramatic, apocalyptic end within forty years, before the close of 1988—or, more precisely, that the "Rapture" would take all Christians to heaven by 1988, leaving the rest of the world behind to suffer and ultimately face the Final Judgment. Two books by the same author were among the many that popularized this view during the latter half of the twentieth century. Titled *On Borrowed Time* and *88 Reasons Why the Rapture Will Be in 1998*, they were reissued in January of 1988 in a two-books-in-one edition that gave readers just months to prepare, since the author assured them that the Rapture would occur between September 13 and September 14 of that year.

Vena emphasizes that Revelation should not be treated as a crystal ball. It was written to speak relevantly to its own generation in words of comfort and warning, not to disclose secrets of a far-off end-time. Hence, when he has John address us, it is not so that John can tell us secrets about our era, coded in Revelation, but to show how things very familiar to us resemble events and practices of John's time. Hence, Revelation speaks to our era not as prediction but by analogy; and this analogizing is possible because human beings repeat themselves generation by generation. In the primary matters of love and hate, justice and injustice, hope and despair, compassion and cruelty, one generation's ways rhyme with those of the next.

One of the most disturbing aspects of the Book of Revelation is the recurrence of divine violence in the visions. Anyone familiar with the ancient world knows that people in John's time took for granted that the gods behave vengefully when they think they have been wronged or disrespected. Many ancient people also assumed that violence against one's own enemies is always justified, whether sanctioned by law or not. The idea that the gods sometimes act violently is found not only among pagans but also in Judaism and Christianity. In the New Testament, forms of this view appear not only in Revelation but also in the gospels and the letters. Hence, the Book of Revelation is not exceptional in its implication that God uses violence to set the world straight.

Most readers of Vena's books probably find the idea of justice through divine violence troubling. In *Postcards from Patmos*, Vena reframes Revelation's visions of divine violence by inviting us to consider what those visions must have meant to those who suffered violence at the hands of other human beings, especially when the sufferers were incapable of avoiding the violence or defending themselves. He also points out that Revelation nowhere encourages Christians to answer violence with violence. The scenes of divine violence are not models to be imitated but cathartic stories that give the suffering readers' own anger a chance to discharge non-violently. It is a kind of purging of justifiable anger.

The concept of catharsis through story goes back to Aristotle's theory of drama. Ancient drama functioned cathartically, Aristotle suggested, not because the events it depicted actually took place but because it gave people an outlet for their emotions, whether of love or hate, longing or despair, or any other intense emotion. As spectators of drama, people discharged their emotions therapeutically, Aristotle believed.

Vena's use of the term "catharsis" for the effect of Revelation does not require that we adopt Aristotle's view or treat Revelation as a kind of dramatic fiction. Rather, it encourages us to consider Aristotle's view as a possible aid to considering how the visions of Revelation may have functioned for its original readers and how they may function in similar or different ways for readers today.

It is this sort of thoughtful engagement with Revelation—an engagement that Vena models and seeks to stimulate in his readers—that makes *Postcards from Patmos* a welcome addition to the church's ongoing wrestling with the difficult, final book of the Bible. And Vena also achieves something that ancient literary connoisseurs deemed the highest art: to write in a way that makes reading both a benefit and a pleasure. John would probably have agreed.

Charles H. Cosgrove
Emeritus Professor of Early Christian Literature
Garrett-Evangelical Theological Seminary

Prologue

IN THIS WORK, A fictionalized John is addressing a contemporary audience directly, as if they were the original recipients of Revelation. Unlike my two previous books, which were historical fictions, this one does not include fictional elements beyond John's knowledge of his reader's time and culture. It does not dwell on possible scenarios advanced by information found in the text, like the trip to Spain in the case of Paul. Rather, it aims to provide a contemporary audience with some additional historical information, so they can have a better understanding of the place and time when John wrote. You will notice, for example, that John uses male language to address God, so instead of using inclusive language, which would be anachronistic, I decided to let him be ancient. I also explore, fictionally, John's feelings, to allow the readers to imagine how he might have felt in the troubled times he lived in. When this happens, the font will be in italics. It is recommended that the reader have a Bible at hand to review the text whenever necessary.

Acknowledgments

I WANT TO ACKNOWLEDGE the influence of several people who contributed to the writing of this book.

My good friend and colleague Al Caldwell, who encouraged me to visit John's world by making many references to Patmos as part of the prophet's identity.

Sophia Twaddell, who by her precise editing and suggestions that fine-tuned the manuscript, made it readable for non-scholarly audiences.

Charles H. Cosgrove, who not only wrote another forward to this series but also confirmed my intuition of keeping John ancient, even when he is addressing a contemporary audience, thus eliminating all-inclusive language when referring to God.

To all of them I will be forever thankful.

Osvaldo D. Vena
September, 2024

Introduction

THE BOOK OF REVELATION, also known as The Revelation to John and the Book of the Apocalypse, is the final book of the New Testament and therefore the final book of the Christian Bible. Written in Koine (common) Greek, its title is derived from the first word of the text: *apokalypsis*, which means "unveiling" or "revelation." It is the only apocalyptic book in the New Testament canon and occupies a central place in Christian eschatology.

People have different attitudes toward Revelation: lack of interest (it is irrelevant), fear (the end is near), embarrassment (its theology is so different from that of Jesus' love for enemies), ignorance (how does one read such a book?) Still some people find pleasure in reading it. They believe that they will not see the catastrophic destruction of the end times because God will rescue them. They are the proponents of the so called "rapture theology" made popular by Hal Lindsey in *The Great Late Planet Earth* and more recently by the *Left Behind* novels by Tim LaHaye and Jerry B. Jenkins.

Revelation has stimulated the formation of sectarian movements such as that of Jim Jones in 1978 or David Koresh in 1993. These people withdrew from society to wait for the end of days.

Many times, they become violent or suicidal, as is the case with the two examples noted above. On the other hand, Revelation has inspired oppressed groups in the Third World to struggle for justice, for they understand this book to be about resisting evil in society. Obviously, there is no consensus as to how to interpret Revelation.

With many other scholars and students of Revelation, I agree that it must be read in its historical and social context, trying to unpack what it meant for the first readers, who lived in First Century Roman dominated Asia Minor. It is only when we know something about the communities that received this message that we can try to relate it to our present situation. Revelation was not written for us. We were not in the author's mind. Besides, the two worlds are so different that we have to make an effort to understand these differences. Otherwise, the message is lost in translation.

What Kind of Book is Revelation?

Revelation belongs to the apocalyptic genre, which was popularized during times of imperial domination (Hellenistic, Roman) and used as literature of resistance, helping people to cope with oppression by presenting a vision of the future where God was going to overcome evil and vindicate God's suffering people. The apocalyptic worldview was dualistic. There was good, and there was evil. There was God, and there was Satan. The present world was dominated by the powers of sin, death and evil, but in a short time these powers were going to be defeated by God and the world would finally arrive to a situation of peace, blessing, and happiness. The message of the apocalyptic literature is that despite what is happening in the world, it is God who is in control of history. That is why it is so important to remain faithful, otherwise God would come to exercise judgment on God's own people.

The language of the apocalyptic literature deserves special attention. It relies on legends and myths that were present in all ancient cultures, including Israel. It was familiar to its first readers. It was the way in which they tried to explain reality in order to give coherence and meaning to their lives. It replaced history in a time when such a concept did not exist; even though it was not "historical," it had historical "relevance." Another technique this language uses is numbers. They have a special meaning that is almost always symbolic rather than literal. For example, number 7 means something whole, perfect. The same idea is present in numbers 3 and 12, while 6 points at something *less* than perfect, and 8 to something *more* than perfect.

Revelation is an example of a Christian apocalypse,[1] and its symbols reflect that reality. Sure enough, beginning with the first chapter, the risen Christ plays a central role in the story. It is Jesus who sends his angel to reveal to John the course of events awaiting the churches to whom John is writing to. The source of the unveiling is God, but it is mediated twice, first through Jesus, then through the angel. The letters to the churches are a direct revelation of Jesus to John. Later, an angel will take him in a heavenly journey. Thus, John uses the apocalyptic genre and christianizes it. This is especially clear in the way he describes the sacrificed Lamb, a reference to Jesus.

But what about the historical context in which it was written? John was given a vision by which he encouraged his community to remain faithful to God without giving in to the demands of the pagan society. In particular, the book of Revelation warns against the practice of the worship of the emperor as divine. Even though it is doubtful that the emperor cult was being enforced on all Christians any time in the first or early second centuries, the audience of Revelation may have been experiencing a partial instance of it under Domitian, and John may have used this practice by some who wanted to flatter the emperor as an excuse to call the Christian community to an intensified exclusiveness over against the Greco Roman culture.

---

1. There is an example of Jewish apocalyptic writing in the Bible: the book of Daniel.

What about Authorship, Date, and Audience?

The text identifies its author as John (1:1,4,9; 22:8), a prophet (1:3; 22:7,10,18,19) who says to be a servant of God (1:1) and a brother sharing in the suffering of the addressees (1:9). John was such a common name at the time that it is impossible to know who is meant here. The author is capitalizing on this fact in order to write a credible work that would be accepted by his audience.

As for the date of the book there are two possibilities: early, during Nero's time (54–68 CE) or late, during Domitian's reign (81–96 CE). In support of an early date, we have two passages: 11:1–3, that describes the temple, which was destroyed by the Romans in 70CE, as still standing, and 13:18, where the number 666 seems to point at "Nero Caesar." Allusions to the return of Nero, in 13:3;17:9–11, and the use of Babylon as a code name for Rome, point to a later date. Revelation was perhaps composed in stages: a first edition comprising 1:4–11 and 4:1—22:5, to which 1:1–3, 1:12—3:22, and 22:6-21 were added in a second edition.[2]

What about the Audience?

The book is addressed to seven small communities of Asia Minor that meet in houses (see Rev 2–3). These congregations are completely immersed in the Greco Roman society and are constantly expected to accept the cultural values of that society, among which the worship of the emperor figured prominently. Either out of fear (we don't want to be seen as antisocial) or out of a sense of immunity (nothing can affect us), many Christians began to participate in social gatherings where libations to the gods and prayers to the emperor were performed. John believes this is a defying act for which they have to repent in order to avoid God's judgment.

It is believed that the fear of being antisocial, even subversive, developed under persecution, both under Nero and Domitian. But Nero's persecution was limited to Christians in and around Rome

2. David E. Aune, *Harper Collins Study Bible* (HarperCollins Publishers: New York, NY) 2087.

and there is no clear historical evidence for Domitian's alleged persecution. The persecution of these Christians was not instigated by any official policy of the Empire but was rather the result of random outbreaks of hostility between Christians and their pagan and Jewish neighbors. We don't know if the persecution actually happened or if the author expected it to happen,[3] in which case it was more prescriptive than descriptive.

There are at least Three Possible Ways of Interpreting Revelation

Contextual: it applies only to John's audience. The problem with this is that Paul's letters are also contextual, but Christians believe that their message is still pertinent.

Futurist: it applies only to the future. It sees history as prophecy being fulfilled. Revelation gives us a blueprint for the future of humans. The problem with this position is that the actual audience is not taken into account, they are just used as a foil to a more contemporary audience.

Typological: the sociopolitical context of Revelation provides a canonical prototype and a utopian language for present situations of injustice and suffering. As one author has put it: "Just as the author of Revelation has used, for example, the Exodus of Israel or the eschatological vision of Ezekiel for giving a prophetic interpretation of his own sociopolitical situation, so do liberation theologians utilize Revelation for the theological interpretation of their own historical situation."[4]

In his book *Apocalypse. A People's Commentary on the Book of Revelation*, Pablo Richard offers some basic guidelines for the interpretation of Revelation from which I extract the following quote as a summary of my own position:

---

3. David E. Aune, *Harper Collins Study Bible*, 2087.

4. Elisabeth Schüssler Fiorenza, *Revelation. Vision of a Just World* (Fortress Press: Minneapolis, MN), 11.

Revelation should be understood in the historical context in which it arose. . .and must be interpreted in the
Spirit in which it was written. . . . The book of Revelation
is not abstract, universal, and eternal, equally valid for
all ages and everywhere. Nor does it contain in enigmatic code form all of history from John to the end of
the world. It is not a news report of the future nor is it
science fiction. We reject every kind of fundamentalist,
dispensationalist, or neoconservative interpretation of
Revelation. We seek to interpret it in a positive manner
in its literal and historical meaning, but we are likewise
striving to interpret our present era in the light of Revelation. That is what we call the spiritual sense of Scripture.[5]

It might be helpful for the reader to have a sense of how this
book has been organized rhetorically. One author, after admitting
that one can find as many outlines of Revelation as there are scholars studying it, proposes her own, utilizing a concentric structure:[6]

a. 1:1–18: Prologue and Epistolary Greeting
  b. 1:9—3:22: Rhetorical Situation in the Cities of Asia Minor
    c. 4:1—9:21; 11:15-19: Opening of the Sealed Scroll: Exodus
        Plagues
      d. 10:1—15:4: The Bitter-Sweet Scroll: "War" against the
          Community
    c'. 15:5—19:10: Exodus from the Oppression of Babylon/Rome
  b'. 19:11—22:9: Liberation from Evil and God's World-City
a'. 22:10-21: Epilogue and Epistolary Frame

These concentric structures, also called "ring compositions,"
make the reader notice the center, in which usually resides the
main idea of the whole paragraph or, as in this case, book. Here,
the war against the oppressed community constitutes the dramatic
center of Revelation. Letters a, b, and c lead to the main idea: the
community is in jeopardy, being assailed by the powers of evil. But
letters a', b', and c' resolve this tension unfolding the final solution:

5. Pablo Richard, *Apocalypse. A People's Commentary on the Book of Revelation* (Orbis: Maryknoll, NY) 3–5.

6. Schüssler Fiorenza, *Revelation*, 35–36.

God will bring deliverance through the creation of a new heaven and a new earth.

Another author, dwelling on Revelation's narrative framework, has proposed an outline that consists of three different stories.[7] I will be using this outline in what follows in the book.

1. Story one: theophany at Patmos, where Jesus is presented as a Majestic Human (1–3).

2. Story two: throne vision in heaven, where Jesus is presented as a Lamb Slain (4–11).

3. Story three: holy war on earth, where Jesus is presented as a Heavenly Warrior (12–22)

I hope this brief introduction has helped you to begin to make sense of a book that has left many people confused. In the body of this work, I will explain many of the details that make up for this confusion. Also, if you would like to pursue this further, you may want to consult some of the many commentaries that have been written, among which are:

Malina, Bruce and Pilch, John J. *Social-Science Commentary on the Book of Revelation*. Minneapolis: MN, Fortress Press, 2000.

Papandrea, James L. *The Wedding of the Lamb. A Historical Approach to the Book of Revelation*. Eugene, OR: Pickwick Publications, 2011.Rhoads, David (editor). *From Every People and Nation. The Book of Revelation in Intercultural Perspective*. Minneapolis: Fortress, 2005.

Richard, Pablo. *Apocalypse: A People's Commentary on the Book of Revelation*. Maryknoll, NY: Orbis, 1995.

Rossing, Barbara R. *The Rapture Exposed. The Message of Hope in the Book of Revelation*. New York: Basic Books, 2004.

Schüssler Fiorenza, Elisabeth. *Revelation. Vision of a Just World*. Minneapolis: Fortress, 1991.

Vena, Osvaldo D. *Apocalipsis*. Minneapolis, MN: Augsburg Fortress, 2005

Witherington, Ben. *Revelation*. The New Cambridge Bible Commentary. Cambridge: University Press, 2003.

Yarbro Collins, Adela. *Crisis and Catharsis: The Power of the Apocalypse*. Philadelphia:Westminster Press, 1984.

---

7. David L. Barr, *New Testament Story. An Introduction* (Wadsworth: Belmont, CA) 436.

I

Jesus, the Majestic Human
(Revelation 1–3)

MY NAME IS JOHANAN (John). As you may know, I lived in Palestine during the first century of our era. I was part of the inner circle of Jesus' disciples, formed also by Peter and his brother Andrew, and James, my brother, because we were the first people he called. We were fishermen, but he summoned us to become fishers of men. Even though at the time we did not understand what that meant, it sounded more exciting than fishing fish, so we followed him. After Jesus died, I joined a community of like believers who began to collect stories about him. Sometime later I put them into writing in what is now known as The Gospel of John. From the same community came three letters. I didn't write them, but they all bear my name because I came to be associated with that group. They were meant to address questions about Jesus' nature (was he human? was he a ghost?) that had emerged in some churches. Finally, I wrote this piece you are reading now, The Apocalypse—which means "revelation,"—as a message from God about the end-times and sent them to seven different churches in Asia Minor. This one I wrote myself. I didn't rely, as before, on oral traditions, but on a vision of the Risen Christ.

I know that people in the 21ˢᵗ century are very skeptical about visions and divine revelations, but in my time, they were very common, though not everyone had them, only those you call mystics. *So, I was a* mystic *and the vision at Patmos was not my first. During Jesus' ministry, Peter, James, and I had a vision of the Risen Christ in a mountain where he transfigured in front of us and acquired divine features.*[1] *And even Jesus had visions. Remember when he was tempted by Satan? Well, that was a vision.*[2] *And what about the apostle Paul? He even admits to having them.*[3] *So, you can see how I am not surprised by visions. And the apocalypse is a long, long vision during which you will be able to see Jesus from three different angles.*[4] *As a Majestic Human,*[5] *as a Lamb that has been slain,*[6] *and as a Heavenly Warrior, ready to conquer.*[7] *But let me start from the beginning:*

In the year 81 after the birth of the Messiah (now you would say 81 Common Era, CE, as a neutral alternative to Anno Domini, AD, which has been traditionally used by Christians but not by Jews) I was in the island of Patmos situated 37 miles south-west of Ephesus in the Aegean Sea, fleeing from the persecution unleashed by the emperor Domitian against Christians. At the time I was almost 70 years old and felt weak and vulnerable, so I decided to leave Judea and find a safer place. I knew that there was a group of exiles living in the island, so I went there with the hopes of ministering to them. I was soon received by some of the brethren, who were anxious to know how things were developing in Judea. I told them that the situation was very bad, and that people had lost their hope because the Lord was not returning from heaven to rescue them as promised. They couldn't understand how it was possible that God would not fulfill His promises, so on top of the physical danger there was also the emotional burden.

1. Cf. Mt 17.1–8; Lk 9:28–36; 2 Pet 1:17–18

2. Mk 1.12–13; Mt 4.1–11; Lk 4.1–13.

3. 2 Cor 12.1–4; 1 Cor 15.3–8; Acts 9.1–9

4. The source for this idea is David Barr, *New Testament Story* (Wadsworth: Belmont, CA, 2002), 436.

5. Chap 1–3.

6. Chap 4–11.

7. Chap 12–22.

I would lie to you if I wouldn't tell you that I felt the same way. Looking for answers, I was in the Spirit on the Lord's Day—that is Sunday—when suddenly I heard behind me a loud voice like a trumpet which commanded me to write in a scroll what I was about to see, and to send it to the seven[8] churches: Ephesus, Smyrna, Pergamum, Thyatira, Sardis, Philadelphia, and Laodicea. I turned around to see whose voice it was that spoke to me, and I saw seven golden lampstands—known as *menorahs*, which have seven branches, one for each day of creation—and in their midst someone like a son of man[9] dressed in a golden robe that reached down to his feet and a golden sash around his chest. Both his head and his hair were white as snow, his eyes like blazing fire, and his feet like bronze glowing in a furnace; and when he spoke it was like the sound of rushing water. He held in his right hand seven stars and a sharp double-edged sword was coming from his mouth. His face was like the sun shining in all its brilliance. I was terrified, and I fell at his feet as though dead. Then he placed his right hand on me and said: "Do not be afraid. I am the First and the Last. I am the Living One; I was dead, and now look, I am alive for ever and ever! And I hold the keys of death and Hades. Write, therefore, what you have seen, what is now and what will take place later."

At this point I realized what was going on. I was having a vision of the Risen Christ! I really did not know what the meaning of the vision was, but he started to explain it to me. He said that the seven stars were the angels, or prophets, of each community and that the seven golden lampstands were the seven churches. Soon after that the vision vanished. I took my pen and a brand-new parchment and began to write the letters, but even though I was doing the writing, the Spirit was telling me what to write. I was not the author but the conduit of the revelation. The Spirit told me to direct all of them to the angels of the churches, but the message

8. The number seven is used 57 times in Revelation, and it symbolizes the divine pattern evident in both the universe and history. David E. Aune, *Harper Collins Study Bible* (HarperCollins Publishers: New York, NY), footnote on Rev 1:4, p. 2089.

9. A human one.

was actually for the communities. Each of the letters starts with a characteristic of the Risen Christ that I had seen in the vision, followed by a commendation to the community for their good work, and a criticism for their bad behavior. Finally, there is a promise to the ones who are victorious.

The first church was Ephesus, the most important city of the Roman province of Asia. Jesus introduces himself as the one who holds the seven stars in his right hand and walks among the seven golden lampstands. This shows that the spirit of Jesus is present and active among all the churches, not only Ephesus. This community receives the approval of the Risen Christ because of its hard work and perseverance. They had rejected wicked people who claimed to be apostles, that is, itinerant missionaries, but who were falsifying the message of the gospel. They also had in their favor their hatred for the practices of the Nicolaitans, people who participated in guilds where the worship of the emperor took place and food sacrificed to idols was consumed. This they did well. But there was something they did wrong: they had stopped loving each other. So, the Risen Christ asks them to consider how far they had fallen and to repent, otherwise he would come and would remove them from their place among the other churches. Of course, they must listen to this message. If they do, they will have the right to eat from the tree of life which is in the paradise of God. And with these words, and this hope, I ended the letter to the Ephesians.

Not knowing the meaning of what I was writing, I started a second letter and addressed it to the church in Smyrna, a city which was one of the most important in Asia Minor, after Ephesus. Jesus introduces himself as the First and the Last, who died and came to life again. It is a brief letter because this church has more positive than negative qualities. Jesus knows their afflictions and poverty but sees these as riches. He knows that they have endured the slander of the Jewish collaborators allied with the empire, who have become a synagogue of Satan. He is about to throw some of them into prison so their faith may be tested. But if they are faithful until death, they will receive from Jesus the crown of life, which is eternal life. I ended the letter by saying that those who listen to the message of the Risen Christ delivered through the Spirit will not suffer the eternal punishment of the wicked.

I addressed the third letter to the church in Pergamum, a city famous for having a hospital and a healing sanctuary dedicated to the Greek god of medicine, Asclepius. Jesus is described as the one who has the sharp two-edged sword in his mouth. This sword was a large sword used for both cutting and piercing.[10] The community is located where Satan has his throne. This might be a reference to the proconsul's judgment seat, or to Pergamum as the center of the imperial cult, or to the Great Altar of Zeus erected there after 230 BCE.[11] Jesus commends them for having kept their faith even when Antipas, one of the members, was killed for being a faithful witness. But Jesus has a few things against this church. For example, there are some members who hold to the teachings of Balaam, who taught Balak to incite the people of Israel to eat food sacrificed to idols and to practice fornication. This comes from the scroll of Moses,[12] where it is told that the Israelites who did that were punished with death by God. But here fornication should not be understood literally, as sexual behavior, but symbolically, as participation in worshipping the emperor. Also, some were following the teachings of the Nicolaitans, whom the Ephesians had rejected. Therefore, they should repent, otherwise Jesus will come to the church soon and will make war against them with the sword of his mouth, that is, the prophetic message, the word of God. Those who listen to what the Spirit is saying to the churches will conquer and will receive from the Risen Christ some of the manna hidden in heaven—a reference to participation in eternal life to which the eucharist maybe a liturgical anticipation—and a white stone. This stone may bear two meanings: one, an invitation to participate in the eschatological banquet; the other, a sort of amulet that works as a permanent protection of the one who wears it, and on which there is written a new name that no one knows except the one who receives it. This new name may be the secret name of God or

10. Witherington III, *Revelation, 102, footnote 86.*

11. David E. Aune, HCSB, 2091.

12. Numbers 25:1–18; 31:1–54.

Christ.[13] At any rate, the two-edge sword and the white stone seem to point at the divisions in the community.

I wrote the fourth letter to the church of Thyatira, a city famous for its textile manufactures and its pottery and bronze artifacts. Jesus introduces himself as the Son of God, whose eyes are like blazing fire and whose feet are like burnished bronze. He knows the community very well. He knows that they are now doing more than what they used to. Still, he has something against them: they tolerate in their midst a woman by the name of Jezebel who calls herself a prophet and who is inciting the members of the church to commit sexual immorality—probably a reference to idolatry, not to actual sexual practices—and to eat food sacrificed to idols, something that took place in the many guilds of the city. The name of this prophetess recalls that of the Canaanite queen of King Ahab of Israel who induced Ahab to worship Canaanite deities.[14] She is also known for her teachings, which the vision calls "Satan's deep secrets," reserved for a few who, because of that, pretended to have a higher standing in the community. Jesus has given her time to repent but she has refused to do it, so he is going to punish her with a sickness that will cast her on a bed, and her followers will be made to suffer, and those who followed her teaching will die. Then all the churches will know that he is the one who searches hearts and minds, and who will repay everyone according to their deeds.

For the rest of the members of the community, who did not hold to her teaching, Jesus has no further requirements, except that they should endure until he comes. When this happens, they will be victorious, and he will give them authority to rule the nations with an iron rod, just as he also received authority from his Father. Now, for you living in the 21st century this language of shattering people to pieces like pottery may seem very violent, but for us, whose lives were constantly being broken by the empire's power, it was a source of consolation. It announced the end of our suffering, even if—as usually was the case—, it never happened. You have a

13. Rev 3:12; 19:12.
14. 1 Kings 18–19; 2 Kings 9.

word for this in your world: cathartic language. It is used to help people get rid of negative emotions so they can continue to live with a certain degree of sanity. The giving of the morning star to the one who is victorious is a veiled reference to the bright planet Venus, which announces the end of the night and the beginning of the new day. It is a sign to the community of their shinning presence in the world.[15] And the letter ends here, with the admonition that they should listen to what the Spirit is saying to the churches.

The fifth letter is to the church in Sardis, the ancient capital of the Seleucid kingdom that arose after the death of Alexander the Great and that was ruled by the Seleucid dynasty. It was built on a rugged hill that protected it from frontal attacks. However, twice in its history had been invaded due to an oversight of the guards who allowed the enemy to enter the city and open the doors from the inside. Jesus introduces himself as the one holding the seven spirits of God and the seven stars. He knows the community, he knows that they have a reputation of being alive, but they are dead. That's why this church receives more exhortations than any of the others: they should wake up—a very pertinent exhortation for a community living in a city with a history of neglect—and strengthen what remains and is about to die, they should remember what they have received and heard, they should hold it fast, and repent. If they do not do that, Jesus will come to them, either presently or at his coming at the end of days, as a thief,[16] and they will not know when. Yet, there are a few people in the church who have not soiled their clothes, that is, they have not committed evil deeds. They will walk with him, dressed in white, possibly a reference to martyrdom ,and their names will not be erased from the book of life (more about this later),[17] but will be acknowledged before the Father and his angels. The letter ends with an invitation, to those who have ears, to hear the message the Spirit is delivering to the churches.

---

15. It is also an epithet of Christ (22.16) and a messianic symbol (Num 24.17; Mt 2.2,10 (Aune, HCSB, 2092).

16. "Thief in the night" is a common metaphor to describe Jesus in the gospels (Mt 24.42–44; Lk 12.39–40).

17. Rev 13.8; 17.8; 20.12,15; 21.27.

The sixth church, Philadelphia, does not receive any reprimands, only promises. The letter starts by Jesus introducing himself as "holy and true" and as the one who holds "the key of David." Because of that, he can open or shut doors as he wants. No one can stop him from doing so. Therefore, he has placed before the church an open door that no one can shut, even though they have little strength. Even so, they have kept his word and have not denied his name. So, he makes the church two promises. One is that those who belong to the synagogue of Satan, a reference perhaps to Jewish collaborators with the empire trying to obtain economic privileges and social prestige, as in the letter to Smyrna, and who claim to be Jews, but they are not, because they do not serve Yahweh but Caesar, will come and fall at their feet recognizing that he has loved the community. The other promise is that because they have kept his command to endure patiently, he will keep them from the hour of trial that is coming on the whole world to test its inhabitants. Jesus affirms that he is coming soon. Because of that they should hold on tight to what they have so no one will be able to take away their crown. The victor will be made a pillar in the temple of God. They will stay there forever, and he will write on them three things: the name of God, the name of the city of God—the New Jerusalem,—and his new name. Here the letter ends, again with an invitation to hear what the Spirit says to the churches.

The seventh and last letter I wrote was to the church in Laodicea, a city famous for its commercial activity and its textile and medical products. Jesus introduces himself as the Amen, the faithful and true witness, and the origin of God's creation. Three characteristics of the city of Laodicea are used to communicate the message to the church: its economic activity, specially banking, its textile industry, famous for producing a black brilliant wool, and a medicine used to cure sicknesses of the eyes. He accuses the church of being lukewarm. Because of that he is about to spit them from his mouth. They believe they are rich, not needing anything, but instead they are poor, blind, and naked. They deserve pity, not praise. The Risen Christ then counsels them to buy from him gold refined in fire, so they can become rich, white clothes, so they can cover their nakedness, and salve for their eyes, so they can see. How being lukewarm—neither cold nor hot,—could be interpreted? One way could be to associate the state of being cold with adherence to the norms of the imperial society and the state of being hot with adherence to the apocalyptic vision of the poor believers of Asia Minor. Not being able to make up their minds between these two completely opposing realities would amount to not being true and faithful witnesses, which would in turn make them lukewarm and sure candidates to be vomited from the mouth of the one True and Faithful Witness. His rebuke and discipline spring from his love for them. That's why, despite all of their faults, he is standing at the door of the community knocking, waiting to be allowed inside. If anyone hears his voice and opens the door he will come and have supper with them, a reference perhaps to the eucharist. To the one who is victorious he will give the right to sit with him on his throne, just as he was victorious and sat with his Father on his throne. The letter ends in the same way as the others, with an invitation to hear the words of the Spirit addressed to the churches.

For you who live in the 21ˢᵗ century the situation of the churches to which these letters are addressed is analogous to the situation of many churches in your time. One thing still remains the same: human desire for power. In the case of the churches in Revelation, this craving for power was embodied in the Roman Empire. In your case, it is in the out-of-control global Market economy. These two systems made demands on Christians which amounted to idolatry, a betrayal of the true God. In my time, people worshiped the emperor as if he were a god. In your time, people worship the market and give in to the demands of consumerism. Blinded by the assumed benefits of capitalism and the democratic system that supports it, some people followed leaders who claimed to be sent by God to deliver them from economic and political deprivation. One of them used Jews as scapegoats and ended up killing six million of them. Another massacred thousands of innocent Palestinians claiming to be doing it in self-defense. Yet another convinced people he could govern despite being unfit to do so on political and moral grounds. And people believed him, especially Christians. And the examples could multiply.

Therefore, the warnings to the church in Revelation are the same for the church in your time: you could be judged by the Risen Christ if you do not remain faithful.

II

Jesus, the Slain Lamb
(Revelation 4–11)

At this point the vision stopped, and I had some time to try to understand what I had written down. But it was impossible. I read my own handwriting, and it was as if it belonged to someone else. The only thing clear to me was that there was a specific message for each of the seven churches, that each of them had good and bad qualities—except Philadelphia, that had only good ones—and that Jesus was coming very soon. Apart from that, the message was very cryptic. But the Risen Christ had not told me to understand it, only to write it and send it to the churches. So, I disposed myself to continue writing but there was no vision, only an overwhelming silence. I soon realized it was the calm before the storm: the prelude to a second vision. And sure enough, the vision came.

I saw an open door in heaven and the voice I had first heard speaking to me like a trumpet told me to come up, because he was going to show me what must take place after this. Suddenly, the Spirit came over me. The island vanished like mist, and suddenly I was in heaven. And there in heaven stood a throne, with someone sitting on it, who looked like jasper and ruby, and around the throne there was a bright green rainbow. Surrounding the throne were twenty-four other thrones and seated on them twenty-four elders dressed in white with crowns of gold. Flashes of lightning, rumbling and peals of thunder were coming from the throne and in front of it there were seven lamps, which are the seven spirits of God, blazing. There was also what looked like a sea of glass, clear as crystal. But there was more. In the center, around the throne, there were four living creatures covered with eyes in front and in back. Each one of them had six wings. The first living creature looked like a lion, the second like an ox, the third like a man, and the fourth like a flying eagle. And they were praising the one sitting on the throne saying:

> "Holy, holy, holy is the Lord God Almighty,
> who was, and is, and is to come."

Then I understood who the one sitting on the throne was. It was God. I was contemplating God's heavenly court! It resembled the emperor's court, where he is used to receive the praise of his subjects, who think of him as a deity. But here it was God, the Creator, not the emperor, who was the object of praise. I realize that for you in the 21st century it is unusual to think in these terms because you don't have emperors anymore. But it is natural for us. It is the only form of government that we know. And so, the vision continued.

Whenever the four living creatures gave God glory, honor, and thanks, the twenty-four elders fell before him and laid their crowns before the throne saying:

> "You are worthy, our Lord and God
> To receive glory and honor and power,
> For you created all things,
> And by your will they were created
> And have their being."

Thinking that the vision couldn't get more awesome, I saw a scroll in the right hand of the one sitting on the throne. It was written on both sides and sealed with seven seals. (The purpose of the seals is to indicate who wrote the document but also to make sure that the proper recipient would open it.)[1] And I saw a mighty angel proclaiming in a loud voice: "Who is worthy to break the seals and open the scroll?" I waited for a while, but no one was found in heaven or on earth or under the earth to be able to do it. I became very upset and began to weep until one of the elders told me to stop, because there was someone able to open the scroll and its seven seals. And who is this one?—I asked. And he answered: "The Lion of the tribe of Judah, the Root of David, he has triumphed and is able to open the scroll and its seals." I looked around hoping to see a Lion but instead I saw a Lamb that appeared to have been slain. It was standing at the center of the throne, encircled by the four living creatures and the elders. It had seven horns, representing kingly power, and seven eyes—the sevenfold Spirit—representing divine omnipresence and omniscience. When it moved toward the one sitting on the throne there was a moment of silence and expectation. Then the Lamb took the scroll from the right hand of the one sitting on the throne and immediately the four living creatures and the twenty-four elders fell before it. Each one had a harp, and they were holding golden bowls full of incense, which represent the prayers of God's people. They seemed to be ready to sing because they took their harps and began to play. And they sang a new song:

> "You are worthy to take the scroll
> and open its seals,
> because you were slain,
> with your blood you purchased for God
> saints from every tribe and language
> and people and nation.
> You have made them to be a kingdom
> and priests to serve our God,
> and they will reign on the earth."

I immediately realized who the Lamb was. I was having another vision of the Risen Christ! They were saying what John the Baptist had said years before when seeing Jesus going by: "Look,

---

1. Witherington, *Revelation*, 119.

the Lamb of God, who takes away the sin of the world!"[2] And when I thought that the singing had ended, I heard the voice of many angels—millions of them—encircling the throne and the living creatures and the elders and singing in a loud voice:

> "Worthy is the Lamb, who was slain,
>> To receive power and wealth and
> Wisdom and strength
>> And honor and glory and praise!"

The whole creation joined this choir: every creature in heaven and on earth and under the earth and on the sea, and all that is in them, were singing. There was no one or nothing left who was not singing. Can you imagine? And they were saying:

> "To him who sits on the throne and to the Lamb
>> Be praise and honor and glory and power,
> For ever and ever!"

The four living creatures gave their consent saying "Amen," and the elders fell again and worshiped God and the Lamb.

What a sight! This may be the prelude to something big, I thought, for even though I was able to understand some of the things that were being said, I did not always grasp their meaning. And I was right. It was the prelude to something amazingly big. It started when the Lamb opened the first of the seven seals and one of the four living creatures said in a voice like thunder, "Come!" I looked and there, in front of me, there was a white horse. Its rider had a bow, and was given a crown, and he rode out determined to conquest. It reminded me of the Parthian Empire, a major Iranian political and cultural power in ancient Iran from 247 BC to 224 AD. They won victories against the Romans on more than one occasion, the last one in 62 CE. They were famous for their horses and their sacred color was white.[3]

The Lamb then opened the second seal, and I heard the second living creature say, "Come!" Immediately, another horse,

---

2. John 1:29.

3. *Revelation*, Ben Witherington III, p.133.

bright red, came out and its rider was allowed to take peace from the earth, so that people would slaughter one another. And he was given a great sword, perhaps a symbol of the empire's power to inflict the death penalty. I thought it was ironic that the rider was allowed to remove peace from the earth. Wasn't the empire supposed to bring peace? I couldn't avoid thinking that the Roman peace, the so-called PAX ROMANA, enforced by the Roman army, was actually the opposite, the absence of peace.

When the Lamb opened the third seal, I heard the third living creature say 'Come!' I looked, and there before me was a black horse. Its rider was holding a pair of scales in his hand. And from the midst of the four living creatures came a voice, saying:

> "Two pounds of wheat for a day's wages,
> And six pounds of barely for a day's wages,
> And do not damage the oil and the wine."

When I understood what the voice was saying I became extremely angry, because it was describing a great injustice. The poor, who depended on wheat and barley for their daily sustenance, could not afford it given the inflationary prices produced by the economic policies of the empire. The price was too high, and they couldn't buy enough food to feed their families with a day's wages. On the other hand, the rich were not affected. They continued to have their extravagant parties in their sumptuous villas, with enough oil and wine that had been cultivated clearing up space otherwise utilized for growing the grains necessary for a peasant's diet.

I know you are familiar with this. It happens still today in the 21ˢᵗ century. An example is the deforestation of the rain forest to make room for raising cattle for the fast-growing fast-food industry. Nothing has changed, you may say, and I agree.

When the Lamb opened the fourth seal the fourth living creature exclaimed: "Come." And there came a pale horse whose rider was named Death, and Hades (the place of the dead) followed him in order to swallow in its bottomless stomach all those who were killed because of the activity of the fourth rider. They were given power over a fourth of the earth to kill by sword, famine, plague, and by the wild beasts of the earth. I was astonished to know the number of people killed by them, but then I remembered the first three seals. There were people dying in each one of them too but for different reasons: the invasion of foreign armies in the first, violent repression by the empire in the second, hunger in the third, and now, those left, were being killed by the fourth rider. Then I understood that the empire was being punished because of its killer nature disguised as peace. The horses and their riders pointed at that.

When the Lamb opened the fifth seal, I saw under the altar the souls of those who had been slain because of the word of God and the testimony of Jesus. They called out in a loud voice saying: "How long, Master, holy and true, until you judge the inhabitants of the earth and avenge our blood?" As an answer each of them was given a white robe, (the symbol of purity), and were told to wait a little longer until the full number of their fellow servants were killed just as they had been. I understood that as meaning that there was a fixed number of martyrs who had to be completed before the end, when the judgment would take place and their blood would be avenged. When I heard these words, I was filled with hope, for I realized that the time of retribution was coming near. But, as you all know, that did not happen. History went on, and those who died did not get revenge. They became martyrs, and many followed in their steps, making martyrdom an indisputable proof of their loyalty to God.

In your own time there are many examples of people who were ready to die for a cause they considered worthwhile: Archbishop Romero of El Salvador, Martin Luther King Jr., and countless others, whose names are not so prominent as to secure a place in the written history, though they have a place in people's hearts.

When he opened the sixth seal, I looked, and there came a cataclysm of cosmic proportions affecting everything: the earth, the sun, the moon, the stars, the heavens—which receded like a scroll being rolled up—and every mountain and island—which were removed from their place. It amounted to a total emptiness, a going back to a pre-creation state! It also affected every human being on earth, from kings, to slaves, to free citizens. Overcome by fear, they hid in caves and mountains wanting to be hidden from the face of the one sitting on the throne and from the wrath of the Lamb, which they knew no one could withstand. The wish of the souls under the altar of the fifth seal seemed to finally have come to its fulfilment. I was hoping to see the end, announced by the prophets[4] and by Paul[5], but I didn't. There was still another seal that needed to be opened, the seventh one. I was expecting the Lamb to open it but instead the vision changed.

After this I saw four angels standing at the four corners of the earth (in my time people believed that the earth was a flat rectangle), holding back the four winds of the earth so that no wind could blow on earth or sea or against any tree. Then I saw another angel ascending from the rising of the sun, having the seal of the living God, and he called out in a loud voice to the four angels who had been given power to damage earth and sea, saying, "Do not damage the earth or the sea or the trees until we have marked the servants of our God with a seal on their foreheads." And I heard the number of those who were sealed, 144,000 from all the tribes of Israel, 12,000 from each one of them: Judah, Reuben, Gad, Asher, Naphtali, Manasseh, Simeon, Levi, Issachar, Zebulun, Joseph, and Benjamin. But I did not see them. What I saw instead was a great multitude that no one could count, from every nation, tribe, people, and language standing before the throne and the Lamb. They were wearing white robes, (symbol of purity, faithfulness, and victory), and holding palm branches in their hands, (also a familiar symbol of victory). They were saying:

> "Salvation belongs to our God,
> who sits on the throne,
> and to the Lamb."

I noticed that they said "belongs", as if it had already happened, as if they were already living the future salvation promised

---

4. Is 13:10; Ez 32:7–8; Jl 2:30–31.

5. 1 Thess 4:13—5:11.

to the righteous ones. On top of that I saw that all the angels, standing around the throne and around the elders and the four living creatures, fell down on their faces before the throne and worshiped God, saying:

> "Amen!
> Praise and glory
> And wisdom and thanks and honor
> And power and strength
> Be to our God for ever and ever.
> Amen!"

That is why I was surprised to hear one of the elders asking me: "These in white robes—who are they, and where did they come from?" I said: Sir, you know. And he answered me: "These are the ones who have come out of the great tribulation; they have washed their robes and made them white in the blood of the Lamb." Even though the imagery was confusing,—how can robes be made white with blood?—I kept listening to the elder).

> "...they are before the throne of God,
> And serve him day and night in his temple;
> And the one who sits on the throne
> will shelter them with his presence.
> They will hunger no more,
> and thirst no more.
> The sun will not strike them,
> Nor any scorching heat.
> For the Lamb at the center of the throne
> will be their shepherd;
> he will lead them to springs of living water.
> And God will wipe away every tear from their eyes."

What an astonishing view of the future for those who survive the great tribulation this was! What can be better than serving God day and night, being sheltered by his presence without experiencing hunger or thirst anymore, being spared the scorching heat of the sun, being led by the Lamb-Shepherd to springs of living water, their tears being wiped away by God. I realized then that I was seeing a preview of heavenly bliss after God's judgment, and that these were the survivors, the chosen ones, the sealed ones.

In my time we divided humanity in Jews and Gentiles, therefore these two groups of people are represented in the heavenly worship: the 144,000 are Jews who believed in Christ, the Lamb; the countless multitude are Gentiles from every nation and tribe who also believed in Christ. They represent God's diverse people on earth. Now, I know that in your time the word tribulation is used differently by different people, and this many times leads to confusion and misunderstanding. Some believe that they will survive the tribulation by being snatched to heaven by God before it occurs, leaving the rest to suffer on earth, even those Christians who did not believe the way they did. These people pretend to have a monopoly on how the end-times ought to be understood and create dissention among the believers. You may know people like these, for example, those who wrote a series of novels entitled The Left Behind that have been read by millions. This kind of theology must be resisted. I hope you will do that.

When the Lamb opened the seventh seal, there was silence in heaven for about half hour. And I saw the seven angels who stand before God, and seven trumpets were given to them. But before they blew their trumpets, another angel, who had a golden censer, came and stood at the altar. He was given much incense to offer with the prayers of all the saints on the golden altar that is before the throne. This reminded me of the golden altar placed in the Jerusalem temple where incense was offered twice a day. The smoke of the incense, together with the prayers of God's people, went up before God from the angel's hand. Then he took the censer and filled it with fire from the altar and threw it on the earth; and there were peals of thunder, rumblings, flashes of lightning, and an earthquake.

At this point the action changed from heaven to earth. So far, I had been informed of things to come. Now, with the trumpets, those things started to happen on earth. Trumpets were used in my time in a very different way than in yours. They were used to announce God's presence in rituals and festivals.[6] Also, as a sign

6. Ex 19:16–19; 20:18; Lev 23:24; 25:9.

for the end-times, when God would come to judge Israel and the nations[7] or would send His anointed one to do so.[8] In this case, they are used to announce the calamities being unfold on earth prior to God's judgment.

Then the seven angels who had the seven trumpets made ready to blow them. The first angel blew his trumpet, and there came hail and fire mixed with blood, and it was hurled down on the earth; and a third of the earth was burned up, as also were a third of the trees and all the green grass. But even though it resembled one of the Egyptian plagues[9] still the damage was not total, only partial.

The second angel blew his trumpet, and something like a great mountain, burning with fire, was thrown into de sea. I immediately recalled the eruption of Vesuvius in 79 CE, which caused the destruction of the city of Pompei. A third of the sea turned into blood,[10] a third of the living creatures in the sea died, and a third of the ships were destroyed. Again, partial damage, not total.

The third angel blew his trumpet and a great star, blazing like a torch, fell from the sky on a third of the rivers and on the springs of water. The name of the star is Wormwood, a reference to a plant famous for its bitter taste, though not poisonous. But here it was, because one third of the waters turned bitter, and many died from the waters that had become bitter. A star falling from the sky may be difficult for you to visualize, unless you think of it as a meteorite, like the one that supposedly fell in Yucatan, Mexico, wiping off the dinosaurs millions of years ago, but for us everything shinny in the skies was a star!

The fourth angel blew his trumpet and a third of the sun, a third of the moon, and a third of the stars were struck and turned dark. As a consequence, a third of the day was kept from shinning, and likewise the night. The purpose was to darken the world by

7. Is 18:3; 27:13; Joel 2:1.
8. Mt 24:31; 1 Cor 15:32; 1 Thess 4:16.
9. Ex 9:22–26.
10. Ex 7:19–21.

targeting its sources of natural light. It reminds us of the plague of darkness that came over Egypt described in the scroll of Moses.[11]

As I watched, I heard an eagle that was flying in midair call out in a loud voice: "Woe! Woe! Woe to the inhabitants of the earth, because of the trumpet blasts about to be sounded by the other three angels." This was something new. The Woes had never occurred before, so this was clearly a warning of the gravity of the events about to be described.

The fifth angel blew his trumpet, and I saw a star that had fallen from the sky to the earth. It was given the key to the shaft of the bottomless pit. In the scroll of David this was the place where God had imprisoned the waters of the original chaos,[12] where Leviathan, the monster who God had defeated at the beginning, was living.[13] That is why it was believed that the Devil and the demons lived there.[14] He opened it, and smoke rose from it like the smoke from a gigantic furnace, darkening the sun and the sky. Then from the smoke came locusts, and they were given authority to behave like scorpions. They were told not to damage the grass or any plant or tree, but only those people who did not have the seal of God on their foreheads. They were not allowed to kill them but only to torture them for five months, which is the life span of a locust. And the agony they suffered was like that of the sting of a scorpion. During those days people will seek death but will not find it; they will long to die, but death will elude them.

In appearance the locusts were like horses equipped for battle. On their heads they wore something like crowns of gold, and their faces resembled human faces. Their hair was like women's hair and their teeth like lions' teeth. They had scales like iron breastplates, and the sound of their wings was like the thundering of many horses and chariots rushing into battle. They had tails with stingers, like scorpions, with the power to torment people for five months. Their king was the angel of the bottomless pit; his name

11. Ex 10:21–23.
12. Psalm 33:7.
13. Psalm 74:14; Isa 27:1.
14. Rom 10:7; 1 Pet 3:19–20.

in Hebrew is Abaddon, and in Greek Apollyon (that is, Destroyer). When I heard this name, I couldn't help to associate it with the god Apollos, whose incarnation Domitian pretended to be. The emperor, who wanted to be worshipped as the savior and peacemaker of the world, was in reality the king of an army of demons whose mission was to torment and to destroy.

The first woe passed. There are still two more woes to come. The sixth angel blew his trumpet, and I heard a voice coming from the four horns of the golden altar that is before God telling him to release the four angels who were bound at the great river Euphrates, a Mesopotamian River symbolizing the enemies of Israel.[15] The fact that they were bound means that they were evil angels who lead demonic armies.[16] When the sixth angel released them they began their macabre task of killing a third of humankind. The number of the troops of cavalry that they led was two hundred million. The riders wore breastplates whose colors were fiery red, dark blue, and yellow as sulfur. The heads of the horses looked like those of lions, and fire and smoke and sulfur came out of their mouths. The power of the horses was in their mouths and in their tales, which were like snakes, having heads with which they inflicted injury. The rest of humankind who were not killed by these plagues, did not repent of the works of their hands, or give up worshipping demons and idols of gold, silver, bronze, stone, and wood, which cannot see or hear or walk. And they did not repent of their murders, sorceries, fornication, and thefts.

I thought that with a third of humankind being killed, people should have realized that God wasn't very happy with their lifestyle and therefore sent the four angels to implement His judgment. Their lifestyle was marked by idolatry, and they should have repented, but they didn't, they continued to worship the idols they had made in a manner very similar to what is told of king Belshazzar in the scroll of the prophet Daniel: he refused to acknowledge, unlike his father Nebuchadnezzar, that there was a God in heaven, but rather persisted in his erroneous practice until his kingdom

15. See Isa 7:20; 8:7; Jer 46:10 (Aune, *HCSB*, 2099).
16. Aune, HCSB, 2099.

was taken from him and given to other people.[17] The other two thirds of humankind, who were not killed by the horses and riders, benefitted so much from complying with the emperor's cult, where he was worshipped as a god, that persisted stubbornly on this practice because it gave them power and social status, and no number of killings was going to make them change their minds.

I suppose that there are people in your world that behave under the same premise of gaining power at any cost, not caring about how this affects their families and friends, not to mention society. Their hearts harden, their consciousness is numbed by the intoxicating allure of power, and the desire for success enthrones the ego in the center of their lives. I understand that you have created many things that have become central to your lives—iPhones, flat TVs, laptops, cars, etc. You made them and now you worship the work of your hands. It is modern idolatry.

Then I saw another mighty angel coming down from heaven. He was wrapped in a cloud and had a rainbow over his head; his face was like the sun, and his legs like pillars of fire. He held a little scroll, which lay open in his hand. He planted his right foot on the sea and his left foot on the land, and he gave a loud shout like the roar of a lion. When he shouted, the voices of the seven thunders spoke, and I was about to write but I heard a voice from heaven telling me to seal up what the seven thunders have said and to not write it down.

Pondering the identity of this mighty angel, I noticed characteristics like those of Christ which I had seen in the first vision: coming down from heaven robed in clouds, his face shinning like the sun, his legs like fiery pillars, and a rainbow above his head. But this was not Christ, this was an angel, and I mighty one at that, for he spoke on behalf of God and the Lamb. Here I was confused again. At the beginning of the vision, I was told to write everything down, but now I was told to stop writing. To write or not to write, that was the question. . .

Then the angel I had seen standing on the sea and on the land raised his right hand to heaven and swore by him who lives for ever and ever, who created the heavens and all that is in them, the

17. Dan 5:23.

earth and all that is in it, and the sea and all that is in it, and said, "There will be no more delay, but in the days when the seventh angel is to blow his trumpet, the mystery of God will be accomplished, just as he announced to his servants the prophets." When I saw this, I realized that what was coming would affect the whole cosmos. The time was ending, the mystery of God was about to be revealed, and I felt very happy because the suffering of God's people was about to end.

Then the voice that I had heard from heaven spoke to me once more, saying, "Go, take the scroll that lies open in the hand of the angel who is standing on the sea and on the land." So I went to the angel and asked him to give me the little scroll. And he said to me, "Take it and eat it. It will turn your stomach sour, but in your mouth, it will be as sweet as honey." I did as he commanded me and ate it, and as he said, it tasted as sweet as honey in my mouth. But when I had eaten it, my stomach turned sour. Then I was told, "You must prophesy again about many peoples, nations, languages and kings."

I was familiar with the book of Ezekiel, where the prophet is given a scroll, symbolizing his prophetic ministry against Israel, and was ordered to eat it, knowing that in his mouth it was going to taste as sweet as honey.[18] *It was the same in my case, except that it turned sour in my stomach. What was the meaning of it? Was it that my ministry was going to cause me more pain than what I already had experienced? I was not ready for this. I thought my prophetic days were going to be over once I delivered this last prophecy, but the angel told me that I was not done yet, that there were many more people, nations, languages, and kings that had to hear the message.*

At this point I think I need to clarify what I mean by prophecy. It is not a prediction of the future, as you may think, a sort of blueprint of what is going to happen until God brings his kingdom. No. It is something very different. It is an indictment on the evil doers, an announcement of the divine judgment that is awaiting them. The prophets condemned Israel's kings for their oppression of the poor, and also the religious hierarchy for their hypocrisy, while at the same

18. Ezekiel 2:8—3:3.

time assured the downtrodden and the faithful that God was going to liberate them. But in my vision the prophecy was not directed to Israel but to the Gentiles of the earth.

Then I was given a measuring rod like a staff, and I was told, "Come and measure the temple of God and the altar, with its worshipers but exclude the outer court; do not measure it, because it has been given to the Gentiles and they will trample over the holy city for 42 months. And I will grant my two witnesses authority to prophecy for 1,260 days, wearing sackcloth."

Now, he couldn't have been referring to the physical temple, for this had been destroyed in 70 CE and I was writing in the 90s. So, what was he talking about when he told me to measure the temple and its worshipers? And what did he mean by measuring? In my understanding, measuring can be a sign of restoration, or protection from physical harm, or preservation from spiritual harm. Notice that I never got to do what I was told, for the vision changed again and two new characters were introduced, "my two witnesses." Who were they? Let's go back to the vision again. It says that they are the two olive trees and the two lampstands that stand before the Lord of the earth and that if anyone wants to harm them, fire comes from their mouths and devours their enemies. They also have the power to close up the heavens so that it will not rain during the time of their prophesying and to turn the waters into blood, and to strike the earth with every kind of plague.

Again, all of this sounded very familiar. In the scroll of Zechariah one can read of two olive trees and two lampstands, just like here. The prophet tells us that they represent Joshua and Zerubbabel, the two heroes of the temple reconstruction after Israel returned from captivity. But they also resembled the prophet Elijah, who announced to king Ahab of a drought that was going to come upon de earth by his every word,[19] and Moses, who made the waters of the Red Sea turn into blood and filled the land of Egypt with all kinds of plagues[20]. As you can see, the symbolism piles up and soon you don't know what the vision really means. But then something happens. The

---

19. 1 Kings 17:1; 18:1.

20. Exodus 7:14–25.

1,260 days of their witness come to a stop, and from being the ones doing the harm, they turn into the ones being harmed, a complete reversal of fortunes, yes, but by now I should have known that this is a recurrent motif of this revelation. What happens next, though, is upsetting. . .They are killed by the beast that comes up from the bottomless pit and their dead bodies will lie in the streets of the great city that prophetically is called Sodom and Egypt, where also their Lord was crucified. For three and a half days members of the peoples and tribes and languages and nations will gaze at their dead bodies and refuse to bury them. They will gloat over them and celebrate, and exchange presents, because these two prophets had been a torment to those who live on the earth.

There are many parallels here between their ministry and that of Jesus. Like them, Jesus too was called a witness[21], was compared to Elijah and Moses,[22] his ministry was considered a torment for some[23], he had the power to perform miracles, was murdered publicly in Jerusalem by imperial power, was risen after three days, and was taken to heaven in a cloud while others looked on.[24] The pattern seems to be one of persecution, martyrdom, resurrection, and glorification. I wonder if the two witnesses are not in fact representing the church, the people of God on earth who carry on their prophetic ministries imitating Jesus. Everything seems to point to that direction, especially when it says that they were killed in the same city where their Lord was crucified, a clear reference to Jerusalem. If that is true, then what follows in the vision does not affect them but the rest of the inhabitants of the earth. Let's listen. . .

The vision says that there was a severe earthquake and a tenth of the city collapsed killing seven thousand people, and the survivors were terrified and gave glory to the God of heaven.

What city is the vision referring to? Jerusalem? Rome? Maybe it is referring figuratively to the whole Roman Empire, the "big city." Notice that some of the survivors give glory to the God of heaven, a

21. Rev 1:5.
22. Mk 8:28; Mt 5:17–48.
23. Mk 1:24; 5:7.
24. Acts 1:9–10.

clear sign of repentance. Even this late in the unfolding of God's plan to judge the world, there are those who can avoid God's judgment by repenting. Now, these people are not part of the church. They are part of the Roman society who worship other gods and goddesses, but who recognize behind all of them an ultimate source to whom now they pay allegiance.

This is akin to what happens in your world today. The church does not have the monopoly of God's saving activity, otherwise it would be controlling God, telling God who should and who should not be saved. But that is not the way it works, to the chagrin of too many Christians. One of the main prerogatives of God is to have mercy upon those he wants to. Is there salvation outside the church, many ask? And the answer is yes, if God wants. What about Christ's sacrifice? Was it all in vain? No, it was not in vain, for people can access this way of salvation through their own religion, as the apostle Paul once said so well: "When Gentiles, who do not possess the law, do instinctively what the law requires, these, though not having the law, are a law to themselves. They show that what the law requires is written on their hearts."[25] I believe this law he is talking about is the law of Christ!

The second woe has passed; the third woe is coming soon. And it did, right away. Here is what happened:

The seventh angel sounded his trumpet, and there were loud voices in heaven, saying:

> "The kingdom of the world has become
> the kingdom of our Lord and of his Messiah,
> and he will reign for ever and ever."

Upon hearing this the twenty-four elders, who were seated on their thrones before God, fell on their faces and worshiped Him, singing:

> "We give thanks to you, Lord God Almighty,
> the One who is and who was,
> because you have taken your great power
> and have begun to reign.
> The nations were angry,

25. Rom 2:14–15.

and your wrath has come.
The time has come for judging the dead,
and for rewarding your servants the prophets
and your people who revere your name,
both great and small—and for destroying those who destroy the earth."

The last note of their song was still sounding in my ears when I saw God's temple in heaven being opened, and within the temple I saw the ark of the covenant. And like before, there came flashes of lightning, rumblings, peals of thunder, an earthquake and a severe hailstorm.

There is a feeling of dejà vous and completion in this part of the vision. Previously, we had seen the heavenly worship where the twenty-four elders also fell on their faces and worshiped God, just like they are doing here now. But whereas there God is described as the One who was, and is, and is to come, here He is described as the One who is and who was, but not as the One who is to come, because this has already happened. He has taken great power and have begun to reign. God's wrath has already come and soon the judgment over the evil ones will take place and the faithful will be rewarded. God lives in an eternal present. He doesn't have past or future. He is the eternal I AM, but when he communicates with people, He has to use human language, otherwise we would not be able to understand Him. So, this is an anticipatory vision. It tells me, and those I am writing to, how the end will be. Knowing how bad things are in the world it brings me consolation in the midst of the despair I was experiencing. I told you at the beginning of this prophecy that I came to Patmos looking for answers. Well, I guess now I have found them: God has not forgotten His people. And even though we cannot see it yet, God has brought history to an end.

This last idea is corroborated by what the vision shows next: God's temple in heaven is opened and also the ark of the covenant within it. But we know that both things are gone, the temple destroyed by the Romans, the ark lost or hidden in some unknown place. Nevertheless, they are present in heaven, where God lives in a never-ending present. In fact, they are the original models out of which the earthly things were made. And what follows is a theophany, that is, a manifestation of God's presence similar to the one at Mount Sinai or at the mount where Jesus was transfigured. Since God does not have a body, he cannot be seen. What we see instead are physical manifestations of his power: lightning, rumblings, peals of thunder, earthquakes, and hailstorms. Through these, God is saying that he is very much alive, that he is not dormant, and that soon things will change forever.

But I want you to notice one of the most important messages of the vision: God will punish the destroyers of the earth, those who have abused creation. God will not allow them to go unpunished. In my time, the big spoilers and abusers were the Romans who, in order to maintain their ostentatious way of life, engaged in an aggressive deforestation to use the wood for their temples and palaces. They also planted vines and olive trees in land that should have been used for more essential foods, such as wheat and barley, products necessary for the sustenance of the poor and the peasants. The lands around the Mediterranean Sea were depleted of their natural resources to satisfy the Roman way of life.

I am wondering who the destroyers of the earth are in your time. I am sure you know them. Well, the message of this prophecy is that God will not allow his creation to be destroyed. I guess this imposes a huge responsibility on you, because since God doesn't have a human body, he cannot interfere in human affairs and change things around unless people do it. He only has you and depends on you to do His work. But, as I say in my gospel, he has not left you alone. He has given you His Holy Spirit,[26] so, in reality, he is changing things around but through you. Even in Israelite history this has been the case. Take for example the exodus from Egypt. It was God who defeated Pharaoh, but he did it through Moses. Or the vindication of the Jews in the book of Esther. It was done through queen Esther and Mordechai. As a matter of fact, God is not even mentioned in that book. And lastly, Jesus would always tell the people he was about to heal that for him to be able to do it they needed to exercise faith. Humans participate in God's creation by taking care of it in the face of many who try to spoil it. It is a huge responsibility!

26. John 14: 15–31.

III

Jesus, the Heavenly Warrior
(Revelation 12–22)

THEN THE VISION CHANGED again. New characters, whom I had not seen before, entered the scene. Things are happening now in heaven, not on earth. There is a cosmic dimension that was absent before. The first character to appear is a woman clothed with the sun. If you read back in this prophecy, you might remember that the one who looked like a human being and who was identified as the Risen Christ, had a face like the sun shining in all its brilliance. That can only mean that he was divine. Here the woman is *clothed* with the sun, meaning she is not divine, but she is *clothed* with divinity. In other words, God protects her. Besides, she is standing on the moon, which speaks of her dominion and power, has a crown of twelve stars, and is pregnant, a symbol of life. She is crying out because she is about to give birth.

Then another sign appeared in heaven: an enormous red dragon with seven heads and ten horns and seven crowns on its heads. Its power rivals that of the woman standing on the moon. In a demonstration of hubris, he sweeps down a third of the stars and throws them to the earth. He is what in your time would be called "a bully." Then he stands before the woman and waits for her to deliver the baby. When she does, the dragon gets furious because she gives birth to a son, a male child who will rule all the nations with an iron scepter. So, he tries to kill him, but the child is taken up to God's throne. There are a couple of images here that need interpretation. Who is the dragon? The vision gives his name: it is that ancient serpent[1] who is called the Devil, or Satan, the deceiver of the whole world. And the woman, who is she?

In my time there was this myth of the Queen of Heaven that appeared in many cultures: Egypt, Greece, Babylon, Asia Minor. It was about a woman who is pregnant and is being accosted by a dragon, symbol of evil or death; but the gods protect her when she gives birth. Here we have something similar: there is a great red dragon with seven heads and ten horns and seven crowns on its heads, the meaning of which is unknown to me now, as it is also the meaning of the crown of twelve stars on the woman's head. But by now I am used to this partial unfolding of the vision. I am sure the meaning will come, and when it does, I will surely let you know.

There are some clues from the writings of the prophets who depict Israel as a woman in labor, exactly like here. So, the woman could be Israel. If so, the crown of twelve stars is a reference to the twelve tribes. But she could also refer to the church, and so the twelve stars refer to the twelve apostles. There is a third possibility though. If the child is the Messiah, and I think it is, then the woman is Mary, Jesus' mother, who came to be known as the queen of heaven. These are all possibilities but, as I said, the revelation is ongoing, it is not finished. I am puzzled by it and trying to make sense out of it. Let's see what happens next. . .

It says that the woman fled into the wilderness to a place prepared for her by God, where she might be taken care of for 1,260 days. All of this sounds very familiar to me, but I still cannot understand it completely. I am aware that it is in the desert where God's people experience liberation. For example, the Moses scroll talks about how Israel was sustained by God with the manna from heaven, and tradition tells us about John the Baptist announcing in the wilderness the approaching time of salvation, and Jesus himself starting his ministry

1. Gen 3:1–7; 2 Cor 11:3.

in the desert after defeating Satan, but none of these examples talk about a woman. There is one example though, again in Moses' writings,[2] of a woman being protected by God in the desert. That woman was Hagar, the Egyptian slave- girl of Sarai, Abram's wife. Sarai was very jealous of her because while she was sterile, Hagar was not. In fact, she had given birth to a son who became Abram's firstborn. Now, the custom in those days was that a man could have descendants through a woman not his wife if she couldn't have children. But the problem was that God had promised Abram descendants regardless of Sarai's condition.[3] When the promise failed to happen, Sarai asked him to follow the custom and provide her with descendants through Hagar, the Egyptian slave. So, Abram complied and slept with Hagar, who conceived and bore a son, Ishmael. When this happened, she started to look down on her mistress on account of her sterility. Finally, Sarai had a son, Isaac. The day on which Isaac was circumcised, Ishmael was making fun of him (I am not sure why, but it is what the scroll says. . .) and this was enough for Sarai. She could perhaps put up with Hagar's arrogant attitude but not with Ishmael's mockery of Isaac, so she mistreated Hagar badly, because Abram gave her the authority to do so. Hagar had no choice but to ran away for her life, literally. She went into the wilderness where she encountered the Angel of the Lord, a personification of God, who made her a counter promise to the one God had made to Abram, and what a promise that was! her offspring was going to be so numerous that they couldn't be counted, while Abram's could, if anyone could count the dust of the earth. Now here I am perplexed again. If you can count, theoretically, Abram's descendants but cannot do the same with Hagar's, doesn't it make Hagar's progeny bigger than Abram's? I will need an extra revelation to understand this. . .

Next, war broke out in heaven. Michael—one of the traditional archangels, often presented as the commander of the host of angels[4] and the intercessor between humans and God—and his angels fought against the dragon and the dragon and his angels

---

2. Gen 16.

3. Gen 15.

4. Dan 10:13; Jude 9 (HCSB, p.2102, footnote on Rev 12:7).

fought back. But they were not strong enough, and they lost their place in heaven, so the great dragon was hurled down to the earth together with his angels. Once on earth he comes after the woman because she had given birth to a male child. He tries to destroy him, but she and her offspring are taken away to the desert and there they are protected by God. But even here the dragon tries to destroy the woman pouring a river from his mouth trying to sweep her away, but the earth itself comes to her rescue swallowing the river into itself. It is here that the dragon becomes very angry and decides that if cannot kill the woman and her child, at least he can kill those who believe the child is the Messiah. So, he wages war against the rest of her offspring—those who keep God's commands and hold fast their testimony of Jesus. Will he succeed? We don't know yet. But let's keep watching.

And now the vision changes again. Two beasts appear, one coming out of the sea, the other out of the earth. And the dragon watches them while standing on the shore of the sea. The beast coming out of the sea is described in a manner that is very similar to the four beasts that in the scroll of Daniel represent four kings.[5] They are portrayed as resembling a lion, a bear, a leopard, and as having ten horns. However, in this new vision, the four beasts have become one that is described in similar terms: it resembles a leopard but has feet like those of a bear and a mouth like that of a lion, and it has ten horns and seven heads, and it is coming out of the sea. We had seen this beast before as coming out of the Abyss,[6] the place where Leviathan, the primordial dragon-like monster who represents the empires that oppressed Israel, and now God's people, lives. The sea is its habitat from which it draws its power. It is not difficult to discern the meaning: it refers to Rome's absolute control of the Great Sea, to such an extent that they called it *Mare Nostrum* (Our Sea). What a preposterous idea! The Mediterranean Sea, as any other sea in the world, does not belong to any empire. It belongs to God. We can use it but never own it.

---

5. Daniel 7:1–8, 17.
6. Rev 9:1; 11:7.

The beast coming from the sea, with its seven heads and ten horns just like the dragon we saw previously,[7] represents Rome and its emperors. The seven heads symbolize seven kings[8] and the ten horns convey the idea of power. Notice the diadems on them: they point at ten kingdoms or kings[9] inferior to the ones represented by the seven heads. The blasphemous names inscribed on them may refer to the titles that the emperors claimed for themselves: "Savior," "Son of God," "Lord," titles that for the faithful could only be applied to God and His Anointed One, the Messiah. They are blasphemous because they are usurping the place that belongs only to God. One of the heads seems to have received a deathblow but suddenly it was healed. This seems to reflect the belief that Nero, the emperor, who committed suicide in 68 C.E., would come back to life as Nero Redivivus leading the Parthians, the archenemies of Rome, into a rebellion against the empire.

The beast, Rome, has received from the dragon, Satan, his power, his throne, and great authority. The world marvels in view of such display of power and worships the dragon and the beast together saying: "Who is like the beast, and who can fight against it?"[10] Here we start seeing a parallelism between the dragon and God and the beast and the Lamb. In the same way that God has given the Lamb authority and power to reign, so also the dragon has given the beast authority and power. To people the empire was invincible. But they do not realize that its power is not its own. It has been given. And even though the empire manages to defeat God's holy people and to extend its authority over the whole world, it is short lived, only three and a half years. But notice the geographical extent of the empire: it encompasses the whole earth, every tribe, people, language, and nation. We are talking about 59 to 76 million souls! I know what you are thinking: the Roman empire, though huge, did not include all the people who lived at the time. There were other empires coexisting with it: Macedonia, The Seleucid Empire and Ptolemaic Egypt, all of

7. Rev 12:3.
8. Rev 17:10.
9. Rev 17:12.
10. Rev 13:4.

them successors of Alexander the Great. The other large empire was Carthage and empires in China and India, but the Romans did not concern themselves with them.

Empires have this capacity of denying anything other than themselves. They have mastered the vice of self-centeredness and sold it as a virtue. They convey a false sense of reality that is accepted as such by the rest of the world. You know exactly what I am talking about because you live in it, in the belly of the beast as it were. The USA, or "America," as they mistakenly call themselves, pretending to own a continent the same way the Romans tried to own a sea, has the same tendency, and even though it disguises itself as a de- mocracy, it betrays imperial traits, which are exported and imitated by the rest of the world. The so-called "American Dream" is not so different from the "Roman Peace." They both offer protection and success to a limited number of people, but make it sound like it is for everybody. More than dreams they are nightmares!

Then I saw a second beast, coming out of the earth. It had two horns like a lamb, but it spoke like a dragon. It exercised all the authority of the first beast on its behalf and made the earth and its inhabitants worship the first beast, whose fatal wound had been healed. And it performed great signs, even causing fire to come down from heaven to the earth in full view of the people. Because of the signs it was given power to perform on behalf of the first beast, it deceived the inhabitants of the earth. It ordered them to set up an image in honor of the beast who was wounded by the sword and yet lived. The second beast was given power to give breath to the image of the first beast, so that the image could speak and cause all who refused to worship the image to be killed. It also forced all people, great and small, rich and poor, free and slave, to receive a mark on their right hands or on their foreheads, so that they could not buy or sell unless they had the mark, which is the name of the beast or the number of its name. This calls for wisdom. Let the person who has insight calculate the number of the beast, for it is the number of a man. That number is 666.

The idea behind the beast that looks like a lamb but speaks like a dragon is that even though it would be easy to confuse its discourse with a Christian discourse, this beast speaks on behalf of Satan. It is possibly a reference to false prophets, similar to those in Mark 13. As a proof of this, we see how in 16:13, 19:20, and 20:10 the beast is called the "false prophet." The vision is confusing because it speaks of two beasts, but each has a different function. The second beast has all the authority of the first beast, who, as we said, represents Rome. It possesses all the imperial authority and, through it, the Devil's. Its mission is to make sure that people obey and worship the first beast. Hence, the second beast is an agent of the first and this one, in turn, is an agent of the Devil. We could describe the activity of the second beast as that of promoting and enforcing the worship of the first beast, that is, the emperor. All of this seems to point at the priests of the imperial cult: they are the ones meant in this mythic description. They accomplish their work through several tricks, such as making fire come down from heaven to earth, like Elijah,[11] compelling people to make an image of the emperor and worship it, giving life to the image, which now can speak, and killing those who refuse to prostrate in front of it. Once they believe this, then they are ready to submit to the authority of the first beast, Rome, and are branded with the sign of the beast or with the number of its name, 666.

I understand that this number has puzzled people in your days and many interpretations have been proposed. For us in the first century it is not that much of a puzzle. We are accustomed to the significance of numbers. In this case the number 666 may refer to a human being. If 7 points at perfection and 8 to more than perfect then 666 points at something less than perfect, something incomplete and evil. Besides, it would imply an intensification of imperfection, of evil, something very appropriate when referring to the beast. Or, others think, it may point at Nero Caesar, the emperor, for when you add the value of each of the letters in his name, but written in the Hebrew language, it amounts to precisely that number: 666. The problem with this theory is that Nero had already died by the time I received the vision, so perhaps the meaning is rather that the empire had acquired bestial characteristics. In support of this idea is the fact

---

11. 1 Kings 18:38.

that the word for "beast," *zerion* in Greek, adds up to 666 when written in Hebrew characters.

The other issue is the branding of people with the name or the number of the beast. This mark enabled them to buy and sell. Without it a person was condemned to total economic isolation. To belong to a commercial or to a profession's society implied participation in pagan liturgies that expected people to offer sacrifices to the divinized emperor. This automatically excluded Christians, who refused to worship him or his image. Since the vision I received did not explain what this mark was, I give you my take: it was either the imperial seal that was placed on legal documents or the image and the name of the emperor that appeared on coins. If that was the case, then the intention behind it was to force people to use the official money instead of the regional one. If someone would try to do this, they would be identified as followers of the Lamb and servants of God[12] and would be harassed, even killed.

I understand that in your time people have tried to find a correlation between the text and reality and have proposed, for example, that the barcode—also known as QR code—that collection of lines and numbers used to ring up your groceries every time you visit the supermarket, and which is mandatory on all products, is the sign of the beast. Some Christians interpret it literally, as referring to an individual, the anti-Christ, who is supposed to appear at the end-times, speeding up Christ's coming to judge the world. For these believers the end-times are already here, and they are waiting for them to materialize. Still others interpret it symbolically. The mark of the beast refers to the out-of-control, heartless capitalist system that has contaminated the whole world deserving God's punishment. Literal or symbolic, it points to the fact that we humans have succeeded in disobeying God's decrees and have brought upon ourselves the consequences of such a disobedience, unless we repent and get right with God.

As for the use of official rather than regional money you have plenty of instances about this. Take for example how the US dollar is used in the whole world as official currency while the regional money

12. Rev 3:12; 7:3.

is considered obsolete. And notice that the face of many American presidents is engraved in them, making them analogous to the Roman emperors. The same could be said of the Euro, which almost all the countries in Europe are using, having abandoned completely their traditional currency.

Remember that in the previous vision the dragon—the Devil—was standing on the shore of the sea waiting for the arrival of the two beasts, its agents of destruction. Here we have the Lamb again, this time standing on Mount Zion, that is, Jerusalem. According to the prophets, Zion is a place of liberation and protection.[13] From this place God, or his Messiah, will reign over all nations and will destroy death forever. Some of my contemporaries have started talking about it as the heavenly Jerusalem, the place where God resides.[14] And it is precisely here where the Lamb is standing. But he is not alone. He comes accompanied by 144,000 bearing God's name on their foreheads. These had appeared previously in the vision[15] representing all of God's people redeemed by the blood of the Lamb. And as a liturgical backdrop to this amazing sight, there appeared a choir of harpists singing a new song which they only knew. The vision describes them as those who did not defile themselves with women but remained virgins. This cannot be a reference to sexual intimacy, for there is no defilement on something God ordered from the very beginning. No, it refers to the contamination of idol worship, idolatry, something the people of Israel, throughout its long history, was constantly being tempted by. This multitude follows the Lamb, they are disciples, just as we who followed the earthly Jesus were, just as you, who try to live according to Jesus' teaching in your world today, are.

But there is more. They have been redeemed from humankind as first fruits to God, which means that they are servants devoted to God, they are martyrs, sacrificial victims. They have been resurrected, as Christ was, and they anticipate the saints' resurrection at the last day. There is no lie in their mouths for, when faced

13. Is 24:23; 25:7–10; Jl 2:32.

14. Heb 12:22; Gal 4:26.

15. Rev 7:3–4.

with execution, they didn't deny their Lord but told the truth: "We are followers of the Lamb", they said, "we do not worship any other god but the God of Israel."

You who live in the 21st century may draw some insight from the vision. I am thinking of two things in particular. First, the only way to overcome personal and structural evil is through the power of love and self-sacrifice. Do not pay attention to those who pretend to water down this message by trying to convince you that you should accommodate to the culture, that you should worship its many idols: global capitalism, technology, the media. All these things promote progress and success for a few, while the rest of the world is made to suffer. If suffering is going to happen it should happen through sacrificial love, not via the whim of the powerful. Second, in the face of dictatorial governments, such as the Roman Empire, you should stand your ground and resist them, as many in your time have already done, among them archbishop Romero of El Salvador. As someone in my future,—your past,—will say: "The blood of martyrs is the seed of the Church."[16]

But now it seems that the time for a showdown between the dragon and the Lamb has arrived! I hold my breath as I wait for the next phase of the revelation. The setting is prepared. The final battle is about to begin.

You'll notice that there are three angels in this section of the vision. Three more will appear later, but let's start with these. They are messengers. The first proclaims the eternal gospel to all the inhabitants of the earth. They need to repent, for the time for God's judgment has arrived. Therefore, they should turn away from idolatry and worship the Creator. The second angel announces the fall of Babylon.[17] We already noticed that it is a reference to Rome. Like Babylon, the reason for the fall of Rome is idolatry, which she imposed on all nations. The image used is fornication which is explained as the wine she has made people drink in her out- of-control passion.[18] The third angel brings another announcement

16. Tertullian.

17. Is 21:9.

18. Jer 51:7–8.

of judgment utilizing again the image of wine, only that this time it has a different meaning. Now it is the wine of God's fury against those who have worshipped the beast and its image. This wine has not been diluted, it is full-strength, unadulterated, and it is made to drink to those who worshiped the beast and its image and were marked with its seal. The strength of God's wine,—God's fury,—is seen in the kind of punishment inflicted on them: they will burn eternally in the presence of the holy angels and the Lamb.

I imagine that it is difficult for you to understand this language of excessive retribution, especially when it refers to God and the Lamb, Jesus Christ. But it doesn't have to be interpreted literally. It can also be understood as cathartic, that is, as emotional release, so people may concentrate on patiently resisting the empire and getting ready to face martyrdom, should that be needed. And if that is the case then it would amount to a blessing, for they will finally rest from their afflictions. This is a common theme in Jesus' message: if one wants to save one's life, one has to be ready to lose it, that is, to die, for true life is that which is found in God's kingdom, not in this world.[19]

A lot of people in my time, as well as in yours, don't like this idea of suffering. Suffering goes completely against human nature. We were not born to suffer but to enjoy life, which was given to us by God. If, as Moses says in his first scroll, God saw that everything he had created was good, how can he wish bad things to happen to his perfect creation. Some would say: "Well, humankind brought it upon themselves when they disobeyed the Creator. Suffering is man's doing, not God's." Well, yes, but you can't tell oppressed individuals, such as women, slaves and children in my world, or women and people living in ghettos in yours, that they are the ones to be blamed for their oppressions! So, what are we talking about when we say "suffering?" We are talking about chosen suffering, the suffering that is motivated by love and self-giving. It is something we impose on ourselves out of love. It is sacrificial love. But let's move on. The vision has not finished yet.

Now the vision changes and I see a personage like a human being, very similar to the one I encountered at the beginning of the

19. Mark 8:34–38.

vision.[20] In that instance I concluded it was a vision of the Risen Christ and now it is the same. He is described as sitting on a white cloud, wearing a golden crown, and holding a sharp sickle in his hand. I understand the white cloud to be reminiscent of the prophet Daniel's portrayal of one like a son of man riding on the clouds of heaven and approaching the Ancient of Days, God.[21] The crown he wears is a symbol of victory and the sickle of the impending judgment that is about to come. This is the culminating moment of human history when Jesus, the Risen Christ, is about to execute God's judgment.

A fourth angel appears, and later two more, all of them out of the temple in heaven, from God's very presence. They bring precise orders that need to be accomplished immediately. Even the Risen Christ has to obey the orders, which come from God. Here, as throughout the vision, Christ is subordinated to God. This is something even Paul, one of my fellow apostles, would say.[22] The angel calls with a loud voice to the one who sits on the cloud to use his sickle and start the reaping of the earth. This symbolizes judgment[23] but also the regathering of the twelve tribes of Israel at the end times.[24]

The first angel told the Risen Christ to reap the earth and he did this in a positive way: he gathered those in the remaining twelve tribes of Israel who had not yet been killed by the beast and took them to God's presence where they joined the 144,000 who were killed for their fidelity to God. But now the reaping of the earth seems to have negative overtones. A fifth angel came out of the temple also carrying a sharp sickle. Then a sixth angel came out from the altar in the temple. This angel is described as having authority over fire, usually a symbol of judgment. He commands the fifth angel to use his sickle and gather the clusters of the vine of the earth because its grapes are ripe. He obeys, and gathering the

20. Rev 1:13.
21. Dan 7:13–14.
22. 1 Cor 15:28.
23. Hos 6:11; Mt 13:30, 39.
24. Mk 4:29; Jn 4:35–38.

vintage of the earth threw it into the great vine press of the wrath of God.

This activity of trampling in the winepress is a symbol the prophets used for divine judgment. We find it in the scrolls of Joel, Isaiah, and Jeremiah.[25] But here it is the Risen Christ who executes this action. If Rome, the great Babylon, makes all the nations drink from the wine of its fornication, that is, idolatry, here Christ makes the great Babylon pay for its idolatrous crimes. And he does it in a violent way that is difficult to understand. Another important datum is the fact that the trampling takes place outside of the city gates. It was there that criminals were crucified so they wouldn't contaminate the city. According to tradition Jesus died in that place.[26] But now it is Rome, the followers of the beast, who are killed outside of the city so they may not pollute it.

When we think about how much blood has been poured in the many wars that my world and yours have seen, it is offensive to think that the one responsible for this carnage is God. One hundred and eighty-two miles long, 322 kilometers in your world, approximately the extension of the land of Palestine, and the height of the blood reaching to a horse's bridle, about two meters high, are both images that constitute a rhetorical exaggeration meant to convey the idea that God's judgment is going to reach everyone. Unpleasant as it may be, yet it is another example of cathartic language which, as we said before, leads to an emotional, subjective release rather than to a real, objective happening.

Who can understand God's mind? Who would dare to disagree with God's decrees? Who would tell God what to do? God might even change his mind and at the end, when history's curtain is about to close, because God is all knowing, for one of those things that will remain a mystery forever, will forgive and have mercy on his people's enemies.[27] *But if that is the case then it is something that the revelation will have to disclose. We must wait. There is still more to come. . .*

25. Joel 3:12; Isa 63:3; Lam 1:15y.

26. Heb 13:12.

27. Rom 9:15; 11:32–36.

What I saw amazed me. Just when I thought that the plagues were over, seven angels appeared with seven more. I said to myself: how much longer can humanity endure God's wrath? Why does he take so long in bringing his judgment on the earth? Is he enjoying this? (I have to confess that I felt very guilty about thinking like that. . .). It seemed as if the vision was repeating itself, saying the same things but in a different way. Confirmation for this was the sea of glass that I had previously seen, and also the four living creatures. I was contemplating again God's throne in heaven! Standing by the sea of glass I noticed a multitude of people who, according to the vision, had not surrendered to the idolatrous demands of the beast. They are holding harps in their hands, and they are singing a song to the Lamb just like they had done before.[28]

But you might ask, why a glassy sea? In the scroll of Moses, we read that the sea represented the chaos over which God triumphed when he created the world.[29] Here the heavenly throne recreates such triumph. God has overcome the power of chaos forever. The saints standing by the sea of glass point at God's people's victory over the beast, its image, and the number of its name. Previously in the vision their victory over Satan had been announced.[30] Now it is their victory over the earthly diabolic powers incarnated in the empire and the cult to the emperor that is affirmed. Therefore, their victory is finally complete. So, they exult God calling him God Almighty and King of the nations. They sing the song of Moses, and the song of the Lamb. But whereas Moses is a servant, or a slave, the Lamb is neither of them. He is the Risen Christ, and though not God himself, he is not a mere mortal, like Moses. He is the Son of God, the Messiah, the one who will bring God's judgment at the end.

Now there is a new twist in the vision. The temple of the tabernacle of witness is open in heaven. Just like the heavenly Jerusalem was truer than the earthly Jerusalem, so also the heavenly tabernacle was truer than the earthly one. The temple had been destroyed by the Romans in 70 CE and the tabernacle's whereabouts

28. Rev 5:8–10.
29. Gen 1:6–8.
30. Rev 12:11.

were unknown. But for those who relied on and believed in visions, such as I, these were mere copies of the original ones, which were in heaven.[31] Suddenly, out of the temple came angels, seven of them, dressed as the son of man I first saw at the beginning of the vision. One of the four living creatures approached them and gave them seven bowls filled with the wrath of God. Immediately the sanctuary was filled with God's glory in the form of a heavy smoke that did not allow anybody to enter the temple until the plagues were ended. The time for worship has stopped. Now is the time for judgment. Everyone in heaven holds their breath in expectation for what is about to unfold on earth. And so, you too, who are reading this revelation in the 21st century, are about to witness the events of the end through this inspired prophecy.

Then I heard a loud voice from the temple saying to the seven angels, 'Go, pour out the seven bowls of God's wrath on the earth.' The first angel went and poured out his bowl on the land, and ugly, festering sores broke out on the people who had the mark of the beast and worshiped its image. The second angel poured out his bowl on the sea, and it turned into blood like that of a dead person, and every living thing in the sea died. The third angel poured out his bowl on the rivers and springs of water, and they became blood.

What is the source of the loud voice from the temple commanding the seven angels to execute God's wrath on the earth? It can't be other than God. The temple has been filled with smoke which represents God's glory. The voice comes from the midst of it. And what about the seven angels? We have seen them before blowing trumpets that foretold seven plagues. Here there are no trumpets but bowls and when they are poured out, they produce the same devastating effects as the trumpets. Again, we have a repetition of catastrophes meant to announce the final judgment on the earth.

Like the first trumpet, the first bowl affects the earth. It reminds us of the plagues unleashed on the Egyptians by Moses. In his scroll, it is written that God ordered him to take soot from the kiln and throw it on the air, after which it became fine dust

31. Heb 8:2; 9:11.

that scattered all over the land of Egypt, causing festering boils and humans and animals.[32] The second bowl, like the second trumpet, affects the sea, turning it into blood, which makes all living creatures in it to die. And the third bowl, similarly to the third trumpet, affects the rivers and springs of water, turning them into blood also. Again, we recall the plagues of Egypt described in the scroll of Moses.[33]

Then I heard the angel in charge of the waters say: "You are just in these judgments, O Holy One, you who are and who were; for they have shed the blood of your holy people and your prophets, and you have given them blood to drink as they deserve." And I heard the altar respond: "Yes, Lord God Almighty, true and just are your judgments".

In the Judeo-Christian tradition, different angels oversee different aspects of de world, as fire,[34] wind,[35] and the abyss.[36] There is also an angel who controls the waters, who here intones a doxology directed to God for his judgment of the world. I notice that something is missing in this doxology. It is the expression "who is to come." This is not necessary anymore because God has already come, his coming is a reality now. The divine retribution is equivalent to human sin. Because people shed the blood of saints and prophets, they deserve to be given blood to drink. You may recall that earlier in the vision the souls of the martyrs under the altar were calling out to God for justice. They were saying: 'Sovereign Lord, holy and true, how long will it be before you judge and avenge our blood on the inhabitants of the earth?' They were told to wait a bit longer until the number of their fellow slaves and of their brothers, who were soon to be killed as they were, would be complete.[37] Well, now from the altar these martyrs answer with a resounding YES, affirming that God's judgments are just.

32. Ex 9:8–11.
33. Ex 7:17–21.
34. Rev 14:18.
35. Rev 7:1.
36. Rev 9:11.
37. Rev 6:11.

The fourth bowl, like the fourth trumpet, affected the stars, in this case the sun, but while there the sun lost part of its power and became colder here it acquires an unusual intensity that burns people. But instead of repenting and glorify God, they curse him. The fifth bowl is poured over the throne of the beast, that is Rome, the place where the power of the empire converges, and consequently its kingdom is covered with darkness. It is like the fifth trumpet, where a darkening of the sun and the sky is mentioned, only that here only darkness is mentioned. (It reminds us also of the plague of darkness in the scroll of Moses.)[38] People's suffering seems to describe more the consequences of the burns produced by the fourth bowl than those of the darkness of the fifth. Notice the mention of their pain and sores and their agony despite which they still refuse to repent.

The sixth angel poured his bowl on the river Euphrates, and it dries up, in preparation for the coming of the kings from the east. (Something similar happens in the sixth trumpet. Four angels are bound at the river Euphrates). As we know, the waters of the Red Sea were parted by God to allow the Israelites to escape Pharaoh's army. When the waters closed in all the Egyptians perished.[39] The waters of the river Jordan were also stopped by God so Joshua and the people could cross over into Canaan.[40] And in the scroll of Isaiah reference is made to the liberation of the people from the Babylonian captivity with images analogous to the passing of the Red Sea.[41] Here the kings from the East may be a reference to the Parthians, who constituted a permanent threat to the empire and who came precisely from the East, from beyond the Euphrates. This hypothetical invasion is interpreted as punishment for the enemies of God's people.

The vision continues now with an interlude equivalent to the one between the sixth and the seven seal[42]and to the one between

38. Ex 10: 21–23.
39. Ex 14:21–22.
40. Jos 3:14–17.
41. Isa 11:15.
42. Rev 7.

the sixth and the seven trumpet.[43] The dragon, the beast, and the false prophet are described as an unholy, satanic trinity, from whose mouths come out impure spirits in the likeness of frogs. Frogs are considered impure, and we are forbidden from eating them. As a matter of fact, one of the plagues listed in scroll of Moses was the plague of frogs.[44] The mission of these spirits is to assemble the kings of the earth for the final battle, which is going to happen unexpectedly, like a thief in the night—a figure of speech used by the earthly Jesus[45] and also by the apostle Paul[46]—on the great day of God Almighty. People are admonished to stay awake and to remain clothed, thus avoiding God's judgment, which is referred to here with the language of nakedness and shame. But even believers are warned likewise. In the message to the church in Sardis[47] they are admonished to repent of their unfinished work, lest the Risen Christ would come in judgment "like a thief." No one is exempt from God's judgment. No even His people.

I understand that in your time the Church has grown to become a world institution, with millions of members and lots of power. Because of that, many believe that they can get away with less-than-holy attitudes and actions. Some are ready to support demagogic governments if their leaders assure them that their way of life will be preserved. They do not care if some of these leaders are morally corrupt as long as they quote scripture and pretend to live by it. I feel sorry for you. The same thing happened in my time. That is why the end of all things was announced to us. But we thought it was going to happen soon, that we were going to be the last generation to see such evil. But we were mistaken. Probably yours is the last generation. But that God only knows. . .

The place to which the impure spirits summon the kings of the earth is called Harmagedon, which in the Hebrew language means "mountain of Meggido." In the scrolls of the Judges and the

---

43. Rev 10-11.
44. Exodus 7:25—8:14.
45. Matt 24:42-44; Lk 12:39-40.
46. I Thes 5:2-3.
47. Rev 3:3.

prophet Zechariah there is a valley with that name, where some famous battles took place.[48] Since this is a vision, and a lot of its meaning is symbolic, here it refers broadly to a place where the enemies of God will be destroyed.

The seventh bowl is poured out into the air and a deafening voice coming from the heavenly sanctuary, from the very throne, exclaims: "It is done." This is God's voice declaring that everything that the bowls have announced has come to pass. And a succession of meteorological phenomena, which always denote the presence of God as well as His judgment, follow.[49] There is a violent earthquake, more violent than any since the beginning of history. Consequently, Rome, the great Babylon, is split in three parts and the cities of the nations are destroyed. Since the cities are the basis for the Greco Roman civilization, this amounts to God's judgment on human history. This judgment is accompanied by a reversed creation, where instead of the primordial elements being assembled to create the continents, these are dispersed, losing their form and becoming amorphous matter.[50] We are in the presence of another theophany, that is, a manifestation of God's presence which makes the whole of creation shake. The description is very similar to what occurred in the sixth seal,[51] but here it acquires a more final characteristic. The voice from heaven has announced that everything has been accomplished but we still do not know the details of God's judgment, which we hope to be told soon. But for the time being we are left in suspense, and so are you, as we continue watching the drama of salvation history being unfolded.

In this part of the vision, we are confronted with more blood than we can digest, and it all comes from God. There is not a hint of mercy on His part, only retribution for people's lack of repentance. In the first bowl, painful sores come upon those who worship the beast's image. In the second, the sea is turned into blood, producing the death of all its creatures. In the third, the same thing happens

48. Judg 5:19; 2 Chron 35:22; Zech 12:11.
49. Rev 8:5; 11:19.
50. Psalm 97:5; Is 40:4; Ezekiel 38:20.
51. Rev 6:12–14.

to the rivers and springs of water, so that people are made to drink blood. In the fourth, they are scorched by the fierce heat coming from the sun. In the fifth, the throne of the beast, the center of imperial Rome, is plunged into darkness and its inhabitants gnaw their teeth in agony. Even so, they still do not repent of their evil deeds. Let me remind you of something I have already told you: this is symbolic language that has as its purpose to relieve the emotional impact caused by these affirmations.

A good example of this is found in the scroll of David. This is what it says: "O daughter Babylon, you devastator! Happy shall they be who pay you back what you have done to us! Happy shall they be who take your little ones and dash them against the rock!"[52] Who can rejoice over the death of children, even if they are our enemies 'children? No one. The vision admonishes us to leave the judgment in God's hands, even if we don't quite understand it, and to occupy our-selves with the present, respecting life and resisting evil nonviolently.

One of the seven angels comes close to me and tells me he will show me the punishment of the great whore who sits by many waters, with whom the kings and inhabitants of the world have committed adultery. And I was carried in the Spirit to the desert where I was able to confirm what the angel had told me: there was a woman sitting not by many waters but on top of a scarlet beast covered with blasphemous names and with seven heads and ten horns. I had seen a similar beast before[53] and wondered if it is the same one, but for the moment I will suspend judgment and keep on listening to the revelation. . .

The woman is dressed in colors similar to the beast's, adorned with precious jewels, and carries in her hand a golden chalice filled with the abominations of her adulteries. She has a mysteri-ous name: "Babylon the great, mother of whores and of the earth's abominations." The tattoos on her forehead indicate the lowest kind of prostitutes, while the jewels she is wearing point at a rich courtesan. And she is drunk with the blood of saints and mar-tyrs. The description has connotations of voyeurism, that is, the

52. Ps 137:8–9.
53. Rev 13:1.

anonymous contemplation of an erotic scene. This upsets me very much, but I suddenly remembered another woman the vision had talked about previously. It was a woman who gave birth to a male child and was taken by God to the desert to avoid the murderous intentions of the dragon, Satan.[54] This woman carried with her the highest honor a woman can have in our society: mother of a male child—which ensured her with progeny—and protected by God. On the other hand, to be a prostitute was the most abhorred role and with less honor. And this is how the city of Rome is being portrayed here.

In the scrolls of the prophets, mention is made of evil cities utilizing the metaphor of prostitution. For example, Tyre,[55] Nineveh,[56] and Babylon which, like the whore in the vision, sat on many waters and had made many nations drink of her wine.[57] Here the name of the woman is precisely that, Babylon, and it refers to Rome. Like its historical counterpart, Rome has destroyed the Jerusalem temple and subjugated the people of Israel. It is also built by a river, the Tiber, just as historical Babylon was built by the Euphrates. The sin par excellence of all empires is hubris, excessive arrogance, to regard themselves as divine and, because of that, beyond any criticism, to believe they have the right to decide on the life and death of all people. That is why the woman is drunk with the blood of the innocent, here perhaps a reference to the martyrs under some of the latest emperors.

Seeing my astonishment the angel asks me why. I don't have an answer, so he goes on to relate to me the mystery of the woman and of the beast. The beast, he says, "once was, now is not, and yet will come up out of the Abyss and go to its destruction." He says this twice so it must be important. This beast may have been powerful, but things are changing now. Its power is diminishing. Only destruction awaits it. But for the time being the inhabitants of the world, those who do not follow the Lamb, marvel at its power.

54. Rev 12:1–6.
55. Ez 27:1–3; Is 23:16–17.
56. Nah 3:4.
57. Jer 51:7.

Next, the angel goes on to interpret the seven heads and the seven horns. Only the one who has wisdom, he says, will be able to decipher the meaning. And I immediately see why: the seven heads are seven hills, but they are also seven kings. The way I understand this is that the seven hills refer to the seven hills on which Rome was built, and the seven kings refer to seven emperors. Five have fallen, one is still in power, and the other has yet to come. And the beast is also a king, the eight one. As you can see, things get complicated. No wonder the angel said that this is for a mind with wisdom!

But who are these kings really? Surveying our recent history there are several possibilities. Since the vision uses symbolic language, it never gives us the actual names of actual kings, so it is up to us to guess the meaning as well as we can. So, here is what I believe: the seven kings are seven Roman emperors, but since the list is extensive the question is where to start. I would start with Julius Caesar in the year 44 BCE and include in it the emperors who were deified by the Roman senate: Augustus, Claudius, Vespasian, and Titus. That makes five of them. The sixth one would be the present one, Domitian, who expects to be worshiped as a god. As for the seventh one I couldn't tell, for he hasn't come yet. Neither has the eight-one. He seems to be an eschatological (that is the word you use for the end times) emperor who some would regard as Nero redivivus, a resurrected nightmare if you want my opinion. But none of this is clear. The angel only assures me that this last one will also perish when the Lord Jesus comes from heaven in judgment.

The interpretation of the ten horns is also enigmatic. They represent ten kings who have not received their kingdom yet but when they do, they will reign briefly together with the beast. Their reigning is only a pretense so they can transfer the power to the beast. Behind this apparent free decision to cede power to the beast it is God who is moving the strings. During their short reign they will fight against the Lamb, but they will be defeated by him.

The angel continued with his explanation. . .The waters upon which the woman sits are peoples and multitudes and nations and languages. This points to the influence of the city of Rome beyond its geographical borders for, after all, the woman is Rome! Despite its influence, the imperial city will be destroyed. The language utilized to describe such destruction is very strong. It describes the rape of the woman by its lovers, similar to what we find in the scroll of Ezekiel[58] and Hosea[59] to talk about God's punishment of Judah and Israel due to their idolatry. This type of sexual assault is common in our culture, though many of us are uncomfortable with it. We wish things would be different. But then we must accept God's dealing with the unrighteous, whether we like it or not. Who are we to question God?

I know that for you in the 21ˢᵗ century this language is very hard to accept. In your world those who commit rape are some of the most hated people and when they do it, they are severely punished by the law. But it is also true that lately people are lowering their standards when it comes to the treatment of women, especially when those people are public figures such as politicians or the rich. They seem to have a completely different set of values. Take for example some of your presidents. One of them tried to redefine the concept of sexual intercourse, limiting it exclusively to penetration. Another got elected even though he was accused of sexual harassment by some of his victims. And the worst of it was that his supporters, many of whom were believers, continued to support them, not seeing any contradiction between their faith and their political choices. The vision I am relating to you is very clear when it says that such a contradiction cannot go unpunished by God, perhaps not in terms of eternal damnation, which seems to be the fate of unbelievers, but in terms of an overwhelming sense of shame when they realize that they have been on the wrong side of history.

Using the coded name Babylon for Rome now the vision moves to describe its fall. It does so by utilizing images from the scriptures about the destruction of foreign cities.[60] The reason for Rome's fall is the idolatry of power and money. She has seduced the nations with her wealth and has invited the kings of the earth to

---

58. Ezek 23:25–30.

59. Hosea 2:3.

60. Ezek 26–27; Is 13–14; Jer 50–51.

participate in the product of her unjust practices, described as excessive luxuries, pleasures, arrogance, and pride. The consequence of this lifestyle is murder and treating people as mere merchandise, as slaves. God's people are exhorted to come out of her so they would not participate in her sin, nor would they be punished together with her inhabitants. It reminds me of what is found in the scrolls of Jeremiah and Isaiah when these prophets told the people of Israel to leave Babylon.[61] It reminds me also of the exodus from Egypt and the destruction of Sodom and Gomorra by fire[62] when God also told His people to get out. Even though I have never been to Rome I heard there are believers who live there. The apostle Paul wrote them a letter and visited them on his way to Spain, so it must have been a community of considerable size. But they were never told to leave the city. But now the vision is doing precisely that. It seems to me that between Paul's time, around 60 to 66 CE, and the present time, something very tragic happened in the city and in the whole empire. It became corrupted and lost the ideals held dearly during the republic. It enthroned kings who called themselves emperors with absolute powers that made some of them think of themselves as gods, as it is happening today under Domitian.

The city's self-perception is mistaken. She thinks of herself as a queen, yet God sees her as a whore and as a widow who has no one to protect her. She thinks of herself as eternal and invincible, yet her demise will happen in just one hour, that is, very quickly. And what is going to be left of her? Almost nothing, a habitat for wild beasts and demons, unfit for human life. No music, no sounds of work, no lamps illuminating the houses, no love making will be found in her, only the blood of her victims.

What does this city represent for you in the 21ˢᵗ century? It is true that for us it referred to the actual city of Rome, but you must interpret this symbolically. It can't represent your Rome, the center of the Roman Catholic Church and a holy site where more than two thousand years of Christian history and traditions have been

61. Is 48:20; Jer 50:8; 51:6, 45.
62. Gen 18–19.

preserved. If for us Rome was synonyms with idolatry for you it is of faith. If for us Rome deserves God's punishment, for you it has obtained His blessing. Therefore, there must be other ways of interpreting this. One way could be seeing Rome/Babylon as any economic system that turns the market into a god who decides who lives and who dies, and the body and soul of human beings into a merchandise that can be sold. The only thing that matters is the needs of those who can afford it. The needs of the poor do not count.

What is the alternative then? It is to see the world from God's perspective. And what is that? It is the perspective of the Lamb that was slain. He is God's model for humanity. It says that only sacrificial love can give meaning and purpose to our lives. And this love is the fundamental principle of the universe. When it disappears, society turns into a nightmare of corruption and blood, as has happened in our days but also in yours. To live as followers of the Risen Christ will entail for you to incarnate in your lives the love of the Lamb that was sacrificed, infusing your institutions with a vision that may recreate the world, turning it into a place of justice and peace.

Now a great multitude, like the one I saw before,[63] appears, shouting: "Hallelujah!" I recognize the word immediately—which means "Praise the Lord"—from having seen it in the scroll of the Psalms of David, though this is the first time I hear it here. The reason for the heavenly worship is that God has judged Babylon (Rome) and has avenged the blood of the martyrs, thus answering their petition.[64] Because they use the word "salvation," they might represent the triumphant people of God living in His presence eternally.[65] This word has clear political connotations. It is used in the context of the emperor's worship, who is considered the savior of humanity. But now that the imperial city, where Caesar resides, has been judged, there is only one savior left deserving glory and power: God.

Next, the twenty-four elders and the four living creatures whom I had seen at the beginning of the vision, reappear,

63. Rev 7:9.
64. Rev 6:10.
65. Rev 7:13–17.

performing the same type of action, that is, falling on their feet and worshiping the One seated on the throne. And from the throne comes a voice, possibly an angel, inviting all people regardless of their social status, to worship God.

Now it's the turn again for the great multitude to extol God. This time they are announcing a great celebration: the wedding of the Lamb and His bride. In the scriptures Israel has always been portrayed as God's bride.[66] In Paul' letters it is always the Church.[67] But here I don't know yet who it is. I guess I should wait for the vision to unfold. For the time being let us concentrate on what we know: the bride is ready, she has been clothed with fine linen, bright and pure, which contrasts with the clothes of the prostitute we have already seen, also made of fine linen, though their colors were purple and scarlet. I think I understand the symbolism here. Whereas purple and scarlet seem to point at the bloodshed in the imperial city, the vision tells us that the color white points at the righteous deeds of the saints.

Participation in the wedding of the Lamb is by invitation only. I have witnessed this myself. When someone who has not received an invitation to a banquet tries to get a place in it, but is discovered, he is thrown out, usually in a very unbecoming way. Humiliated and scorned he has to leave the banquet hall amongst the laughs of the guests. The angel said that those who have been invited to the wedding of Lamb should considered themselves blessed, that is, worthy of being congratulated. And he added: "These are the true words of God." Realizing then that these words came directly from God I tried to worship the angel but was reprimanded, for it would have been as erroneous to worship this heavenly being as to worship the beast and its image. He said he was a fellow servant with me and the rest of the believers, all of us holding to the testimony of Jesus, that is, the gospel. And then he added these important words: "For the testimony of Jesus is the spirit of prophecy." What does that really mean? It means that the testimony of Jesus, the

66. Hos 2:19; Is 54:5–7.

67. Eph 5:25–33; 2 Cor 11:2.

message of the gospel, is prophetic, that is, it communicates God's will to the world in which the faith communities live.

But before the marriage of the Lamb can be consummated, His enemies must be destroyed. Again, as before in the vision,[68] I saw heaven open and there appeared a rider on a white horse. I thought I had seen him before and probably I had but this one stroked me for the many names he bore: "Faithful and True," "King of kings and Lord of lords," "The Word of God." And he even had a fourth name written on him that nobody knows except himself. The way in which he was described was also very familiar to me: eyes like blazing fire, many crowns on his head, and a sharp sword coming out of his mouth. And then I dawned on me. Yes, I had seen this personage before, at the beginning of the vision. It is the Risen Christ! But there is some new information. The rider is dressed in a robe dipped in blood. But whose blood? His own? His enemies'? In the scroll of Isaiah there is a portrayal of the warrior Yahweh who gets his clothes stained with the blood of his enemies.[69] I wonder if this is the way to interpret this image. I prefer thinking that here the vision refers to Christ's own blood. Why do I say so? Well, because even though the vision utilizes apocalyptic language full of violent imagery here it seems to do the opposite. The Rider strikes the nations with the sword of his mouth, that is, the gospel; the blood on his robe is his own and the fine linen of the heavenly armies that follow him suggests that these are martyrs who have cleansed their garments with the blood of the Lamb. The Word of God judges the world, and the slaughtered Lamb is the one who overcomes the power of the empire and death. The irony is remarkable. The language is very violent, war-like, but the message is non-violent. It is the word of God, the prophetic word, the gospel message that transforms people, not the military power of any empire. As in many other parts of the vision, one expects to see one thing but sees another.

Another angel takes up the stage now, this time standing in the sun, crying with a loud voice, and inviting all the birds that fly

68. Rev 4:1.

69. Is 63:1–6.

in midheaven for the great supper of God. Notice that he is not inviting people to the banquet of the marriage of the Lamb but birds of prey to a banquet of corpses of kings and captains, of the mighty, of horses and their riders, and of people of all possible social conditions. This apparently is the outcome of the battle between Christ and his army and the beast and the kings of the earth. I try to visualize it and it repulses me and makes me sick. But then I realize that there is no battle! The vision simply says that the beast and the false prophet are captured and thrown alive into the lake of fire, a place of eternal punishment located not in the underworld but in the presence of the Lamb.[70]And what about the people? Are they also thrown into the fiery lake? No, they are killed with the sword coming out of the mouth of the rider. But we have already said that this sword represents the gospel, so the killing should be interpreted symbolically. Christ defeats the beast and its minions without shedding a single drop of blood, except his own. For the communities I am writing to, this is a clear indication that the message proclaimed by Jesus, who is the logos (word) of God, will judge the powers of evil and will defeat them. They contemplate, as if it were a movie of your time, the final defeat of Rome and its imperial cult, and are encouraged to keep on living as disciples of the Lamb in the world of the beast.

With the description of the defeat of the beast and its army it would appear that the vision has come to an end. But it has not. There is still more to come. I see another angel coming down from heaven holding in his hand the key to the bottomless pit and a great chain. He seizes Satan—a.k.a. the dragon and the serpent—and binds him for a thousand years, a millennium, an expression which I cannot find anywhere in the scriptures. Then he proceeds to throw him into the pit, which he then locks and seals to prevent him from deceiving the nations anymore until the one thousand years are ended. After that he must be let out for a little while. The bottomless pit is the place from where the locusts had emerged during the blow of the fifth trumpet.[71] It is the place of demons

70. Rev 14:10.
71. Rev 9:1–11.

and death. There is where Satan is sent, to his place, until God will allow him to leave.

Next, I see thrones, and those sitting upon them are given authority to judge. This is not the first time we have seen thrones in heaven.[72] Previously, when the seventh trumpet blew, there were twenty-four elders sitting on thrones, worshiping God and saying that the time for judging the dead, for rewarding God's servants, the prophets, and for destroying those who destroy the earth had come.[73] I also recall the beginning of the vision, where those who conquer are promised to sit with the Risen Christ on his throne.[74] That is precisely what is happening here now: the saints are resurrected and reign with Christ for one thousand years, while the evil ones are being destroyed in the lake of fire. I think that those who sit on the thrones are the elders we saw before. They represent Israel and the Church. God's people, through their representatives, judge the world, which is what the apostle Paul had said:

> "Do you not know that the saints will judge the world? . . .
> Do you not know that we are to judge angels?[75]

If the scene of the thrones and the millennial kingdom takes place in heaven, Satan's release from his prison happens on earth. He is intent on gathering the nations enemies of God represented by Gog and Magog.[76] These names are symbolic and do not refer to any nation in particular, not now, not before, not ever. Notice that they are as numerous as the sand of the sea and that they are scattered around the four corners of the earth. They surround the camp of the saints and the city of Jerusalem. In the scroll of Ezekiel, we find a description of the defeat of Gog, a chief prince among many other rulers.[77] At the time, Israel lived securely in the land without the protection of walled cities. This apparent weakness is

72. Rev 4: 2,4; 11:16.
73. Rev 11:18.
74. Rev 3:21.
75. 1 Cor 6:2–3.
76. Ezek 38–39.
77. Ezek 38:1–3.

taken advantage of by Gog who then decides to attack. But it never gets to do it because God comes to rescue His people, inflicting a total and final victory over Gog by sending fire from heaven.[78] The same thing happens here. The enemies of God are defeated, and the Devil, who had deceived them, is thrown into the lake of fire and sulfur, where the beast and the false prophet are waiting for him to be tormented forever.

At the beginning of the vision, I recall seeing a great throne in heaven with someone, who couldn't have been other than God, sitting on it.[79] The throne reappears here. This time it is white and again it is God who occupies it. This is obvious because all the dead, great and small, that is, all the human race brought back to life, are standing in front of it waiting for God's judgment. But the saints are not part of this judgment. They have already been resurrected and have been reigning with Christ for one thousand years. That was the first resurrection. They only died once. But the ones mentioned here are the ones who have been resurrected for their judgment. They come from many different places: from the earth, from below the earth (Hades), from the sea. In a second, we have this great multitude of undead standing before the throne, waiting for the divine verdict.

At that point two sets of books are opened. In the first set everything that people have done is recorded. I remember reading this in the scroll of Daniel.[80] And even the apostle Paul says something similar.[81] Behind it is the idea that God, who is just, will reward good and punish evil. As for the book of life, the second set, I recall seeing it in the vision always in connection with the righteous. For example, the unpolluted faithful of the community at Sardis had their names written in this book and will be recognized by Jesus at the last judgment.[82] Also, the beast that came from the sea is worshipped by everyone except by those whose names had been written from the foundation of the world in the

78. Ezek 38:8,11,14.
79. Rev 4:2–1.
80. Dan 7:10.
81. 1 Cor 3:10–15; 2 Cor 5:10.
82. Rev 3:5.

book of life of the Lamb that was slaughtered.[83] Finally, when the vision showed a woman riding on a scarlet beast, it says that only those whose names were not written in this book from the beginning of the world were amazed at their sight.[84] The book of life, then, is the book in which the names of all the people who have been faithful to Jesus and to God are written. It is their faithfulness, not their works, that which qualifies them to be inscribed there. They were given the opportunity to repent, and they took it, as were also the unfaithful ones, who rejected it. They persisted on acting wickedly and received the just retribution for their actions. A fine equilibrium between human responsibility and God's grace needs to be always maintained and this is what these two different types of books are pointing at.

The vision ends with everyone being thrown into the fiery lake, what the angel calls the second death, from which there is no resurrection, no hope. There is only one more thing to happen: the marriage of the Lamb. Now we will know who his bride is!

A voice from the throne, God's voice, spoke to me about making all things new, a "new heaven and a new earth." I thought I had heard this before. And yes, I had, in the scroll of Isaiah. I still remember it:

> "For I am about to create new heavens and a new earth;
> the former things shall not be remembered or come to
> mind."[85]

But, I thought, if this is a new creation, one that replaces the old one, where is the sea? Throughout scripture the sea has always been the place inhabited by the enemies of God, a symbol for the primordial chaos. But now that the Devil has been defeated there is no more chaos. And then I saw it. I saw the bride of the Lamb. Finally! It is Jerusalem, the Holy City, coming down from heaven, prepared as a bride adorned for her husband. I had an intuition about this, but I wasn't sure. Now it is confirmed. Jerusalem is the place where God

83. Rev 13:8.
84. Rev 17:8.
85. Isaiah 65:17.

will dwell with His people forever. In it they will receive God's tender loving care: no more tears, no more death, no more mourning and crying. Everything will be new. God has done it, and it will not be reversed. You can imagine how happy I felt knowing that the empire of the beast was over. God, the Alpha and the Omega, the Beginning and the End, has rewarded His children and punished the evil ones, consigning them to the fiery lake together with the Devil and the beasts. I feel sorry for them, but nothing can be done to undo what God in His wisdom has decreed since the beginning of creation. But I wanted to know more about the bride, the Holy City, so I kept listening and soon my curiosity was satisfied.

One of the angels took me in the spirit to a high mountain where I witnessed the descent of the New Jerusalem from heaven. What a view! I was moved to tears knowing that the earthly Jerusalem laid in ruins, destroyed by the Romans. But now things are different. First of all, you should notice that the city comes down to earth, not the other way around. God comes to live among His people. Ever since we can remember the heavenly Jerusalem had been a model of the earthly one, but now that creation has been reinstated there is no need for the Holy City to stay in heaven. Its place is on earth because Creation is now at peace with God's people. Humans and God can now relate to each other the way they used to in Eden.

The first thing that is described are its gates. There are twelve in total, each made of a single pearl, each guarded by an angel. The main street was made of pure gold,—as was the city itself—transparent as glass. The wall was built of jasper. There is no temple in the city yet the glory of God is in it. In the earthly Jerusalem the glory of God was inside the temple. But since there is no temple in the New Jerusalem because God and the Lamb live in it, then the glory of God is not limited to a space but fills in everything. This explains why there is no night or day and why its gates are always open, there is no need to close them at night as in our cities today. This facilitates the coming and going of those who come to pay tribute to God. Therefore, the city without a temple is a sort of temple for the rest of humankind, and its inhabitants officiate as priests, having free and direct access to God and the Lamb. As the bride of the Lamb, it is more than a *physical building. It is a community, the community of the redeemed ones. On its wall the twelve tribes of Israel are represented, and on its foundations the twelve apostles.*

Then the angel proceeded to show me the river of the water of life flowing from the throne of God and of the Lamb, located at the very center of the city. The water of the river is bright as crystal, which contrasts with other rivers I have seen previously in the vision. For example, when the third angel blew his trumpet, a great star blazing like a torch fell from heaven on a third of the rivers and made them poisonous so that many people died from it. Also, when the third angel poured his bowl into the rivers and springs of water they became blood. But here the water is pure and clear and produces life, not death, and it irrigates the tree of life, which grows on either side of the river. This is a very distinct tree indeed, very similar to the ones described in the scroll of Ezekiel, where we read of trees bearing fresh fruit every month and their leaves being used for healing.[86] The prophet was looking for the day when God would establish a new world. Well, that is happening now. He didn't know it, but he was foreseeing our world!

Nothing accursed will be found in the city, says the vision. God's people will worship Him, and they will see His face. It is not difficult to see what the vision intends to convey. It is a sort of inverted Eden. Everything that went wrong there, functions perfectly here: whereas in the garden God prohibited the first couple to eat from the tree of life so they would not live forever, here the fruits of the tree of life are used as nourishment, and its leaves are used as healing for the nations; whereas in Eden God cursed the serpent for having tempted the first couple, and cursed the earth as a consequence of their sin, here it says that there should be no more curses; whereas in Eden Adam and Eve hid themselves from God's presence, ashamed of their nakedness, here the people of God are permanently in communion with Him; whereas in the garden God had to throw them out, here the redeemed ones reign with God for all eternity; whereas in Eden the serpent deceived the first humans, in the New Jerusalem there is no serpent, for it has been destroyed in the lake of fire. Summarizing

---

86. Ezekiel 47:12.

then, similar to the way that in the scroll of Moses, after the first creation, God places the first couple in the garden from where they are thrown out as a consequence of their sin, in the vision I received, after the second creation, God makes the New Jerusalem come down from heaven, and the redeemed ones are to live in it forever, free from sin and its consequence, death, for this has also been defeated.

But in all this it is important to remember that here we are talking about a city, not a garden. Eden speaks of an idyllic situation where humans are placed to cultivate and take care of it. God is the one who plants the garden, not humans.[87] Instead, the New Jerusalem is a city, symbol of human activity, of history. Therefore, history is important. It does not end with the coming of the New Jerusalem. It continues, but with a new orientation. We could say that God borrows the human concept of the city and redeems it, taking away its negative elements of suffering and exploitation for what cities are famous for. But at the same time, He values the positive elements of the city, different people living together side by side and learning from each other, for He makes it His eternal habitation.

87. Gn 2:8.

Epilogue

AND SO, THE VISION arrives at its end. The epilogue resembles the prologue: I am alone in front of the angel. But I am going to hear other voices to. Soon the dialogue will turn into a conversation and, towards the end, into a liturgy. I noticed right away how the names of God and Jesus are used interchangeably. First it is God who has sent His angel and later it is Jesus who does so. It is not the first time that this overlapping occurs. For example, at the beginning of the vision, it is God who identifies Himself as the Alpha and the Omega. Here it is Jesus who makes that affirmation announcing his coming and pronouncing a blessing on those who keep the words of the prophecy spoken through the vision.

I tried to worship Jesus but then the vision changed and now it was the angel who stood in front of me. The heavenly messenger told me not to do that, that I should only worship God. He also told me not to seal up the words of the prophecy, for this was not a time for secrecy but for revelation, for the end was near. Now we know what God is about to do and people should know that too. Still, they have the right to respond to it in the manner they please: some will continue to commit evil deeds, some will continue to live in impurity, but the righteous will keep on doing what is good and living in holiness.

And then Jesus spoke to me again. He announced his coming, which was going to happen soon, and declared blessed the martyrs who had gone through the great tribulation. He issued also an invitation to the ones who are thirsty to drink the water of life, which here is coded language to speak about the Lord's supper. As we participate in this holy meal, we anticipate the Lord's coming. The whole liturgy ends with the formula "Come, Lord Jesus." And then the vision ends in the same way it had started, that is, invoking the grace of the Lord Jesus over all the believers.[1]

I am still waiting for the Lord's coming and so are you in the 21st century. I cannot help it but think that this delay was part of God's plan from the very beginning built into the fabric of the end times so we may remain faithful. This delay can only be understood from a human point of view. God's concept of time is very different. He doesn't have past or future. He lives in a constant present. The apostle Peter in one of his letters says it well:

> *"But do not ignore this one fact, beloved, that with the Lord one day is like a thousand years, and a thousand years are like one day.*
> *The Lord is not slow about his promise, as some think of slowness,*
> *but is patient with you, not wanting any to perish, but all to come to repentance."[2]*

The Lord has also given me an insight into your world, that is why I am able to know certain things about your times. I know for example that many Christians will try to predict the Lord's coming and will fail, not paying attention at what is written in the scroll of Mark, that says that nobody knows the day or the hour of his coming, not even the angels in heaven, nor the Son, but only the Father.[3] People who do that are trying to attract attention to their way of understanding the faith, what you call "theology." The way I see it is

1. Rev 1:4–5.
2. 2 Peter 3:8–9.
3. Mark 13:32G.

that they will follow the beast and the devil into the lake of fire, for they purposely deceived the innocent. But that is my understanding. I know you don't believe in beasts or fiery lakes. You are more prone to believe that punishment is something people inflict on themselves by their very actions, that every deed, thought, and word has a consequence, that we reap what we sowed, and that God is allowing us to exercise our free will without interfering.[4]

The coming of the Lord Jesus will make explicit that which is implicit today in the lives of our communities around the world. That is why instead of discussing dates and final battles we should be engaged in loving our neighbors and resisting evil. The belief in the coming of Jesus should not be the end but the beginning of our Christian praxis.

So, with the last words of the vision I return to my work of helping the communities to withstand the oppression of the Roman Empire, knowing that its days are numbered. But there is still much work to be done. I hope that you, in the 21st. century, will do the same.

AMEN, COME, LORD JESUS!

4. Similar to the Indian concept of karma that refers to an action, work, or deed, and its effect or consequences.

Afterword

READING THE BOOK OF Revelation was part of my devotional life in the years before having access to critical thinking. Encouraged by authors who described the end-times as fast approaching, I would read it against the backdrop of current events and believed that indeed the end was coming. This belief was shared by all the members of my conservative church, so I felt justified and reassured.

People have different attitudes toward Revelation: lack of interest (it is irrelevant), fear (the end is near), embarrassment (its theology is so different from that of Jesus' love for enemies), ignorance (how does one read such a book?) Still some people find pleasure in reading it. They believe that they will not see the catastrophic destruction of the end times because God will rescue them. They are the proponents of the so called "rapture theology" made popular by Hal Lindsey in *The Great Late Planet Earth* and more recently by the *Left Behind* novels by Tim LaHaye and Jerry B. Jenkins.

Revelation has stimulated the formation of sectarian movements such as that of Jim Jones in 1978 or David Koresh in 1993. These people withdrew from society to wait for the end of days. Many times, they become violent or suicidal, as is the case with the two examples noted above. On the other hand, Revelation has inspired oppressed groups in the Third World to struggle for justice, for they understand this book to be about resisting evil in society. Obviously, there is no consensus as to how to interpret Revelation.

With many other scholars and students of Revelation, I agree that it must be read in its historical and social context, trying to unpack what it meant for the first readers, who lived in First Century Roman dominated Asia Minor. It is only when we know something about the communities that received this message that we can try to relate it to our present situation. Revelation was not written for us. We were not in the author's mind. Besides, the two worlds are so different that we must make an effort at understanding them. In this book, I have tried to do so by means of a fictional account that would make the transition simpler. Otherwise, the message would be lost in translation.

Bibliography

Aune, David E. *Harper Collins Study Bible*. New York: HarperCollins, 2006.

Barr, David. *New Testament Story*. Belmont, CA: Wadsworth, 2002.

Malina, Bruce and Pilch, John J. *Social-Science Commentary on the Book of Revelation*. Minneapolis: MN, Fortress Press, 2000.

Papandrea, James L. *The Wedding of the Lamb. A Historical Approach to the Book of Revelation*. Eugene, OR: Pickwick Publications, 2011.

Rhoads, David (editor). *From Every People and Nation. The Book of Revelation in Intercultural Perspective*. Minneapolis: Fortress, 2005.

Richard, Pablo. *Apocalypse: A People's Commentary on the Book of Revelation*. Maryknoll, NY: Orbis, 1995.

Rossing, Barbara R. *The Rapture Exposed. The Message of Hope in the Book of Revelation*. New York: Basic Books, 2004.

Schüssler Fiorenza, Elisabeth. *Revelation. Vision of a Just World*. Minneapolis: Fortress, 1991.

Vena, Osvaldo D. *Apocalipsis*. Minneapolis, MN: Augsburg Fortress, 2005

Witherington, Ben. *Revelation. The New Cambridge Bible Commentary*. Cambridge: University Press, 2003.

Yarbro Collins, Adela. *Crisis and Catharsis: The Power of the Apocalypse*. Philadelphia:Westminster Press, 1984.